KEVIN WIGNALL

PEOPLE
DIE

A NOVEL

SIMON & SCHUSTER
NEW YORK LONDON TORONTO SYDNEY SINGAPORE

SIMON & SCHUSTER
Rockefeller Center
1230 Avenue of the Americas
New York, NY 10020

Originally published in Great Britain in 2001 by Hodder and Stoughton
A division of Hodder Headline

Designed by Karolina Harris

Manufactured in the United States of America

ISBN 978-1-5011-1941-5

FOR MY PARENTS AND BROTHERS

"BORN LUCKY"

ACKNOWLEDGMENTS

I'd like to thank my agent, Jonny Geller. I'd also like to thank Jon Wood for making the editorial process such a smooth one. And finally, I tip my hat to the one who got away—you know who you are.

JJ hesitated at the door. He could hear a voice in the room and stopped to listen but realized after just a few seconds that Bostridge was talking to a prostitute. He was talking his way through putting on a condom, the strange reassuring tones middle-aged men seemed to fall into when they were in bed with young women, all guilt and denial and embarrassment.

So much for the information. Viner had stressed one thing above all about Bostridge, that he was a real family man, never played away from home, that he'd definitely be on his own at that time of the evening. And Viner of all people should have known better, the messy unpredictable ways people went about getting sex.

He eased the lock and walked in—a large room running to darkness at the edges, pockets of light, one of them around the bed. Bostridge was kissing her on the neck and shoulder like it was something he'd seen in some "better lovemaking" video. He clearly hadn't heard JJ come in. She saw him straight away though, and moved awkwardly, at first earning more misplaced reassurance before Bostridge too realized there was someone else with them.

He glanced across the room and saw JJ and then sprang away from her, almost comically, as if trying to suggest the two of them were just sharing the bed. It was typical of men like him, to move instinctively away from the one thing he might have used as a shield against the bullets. Not that it would have made any difference in this case.

JJ put one through his heart, another in his head, the silencer producing two concentrated little sneezes that seemed to stop the clocks. For a while the three of them were suspended there in the cozy fabric-light of the table lamps, like a tableau in a wax museum, the moment captured for people to speculate on what might have happened before or after, and on the characters: heartless killer, hapless victim, the girl between.

It was the girl who moved first, sliding calmly from the bed without looking at either of them. He was taken aback by how young she looked, easily still in her teens, corn blond hair cut boyish, loose limbs, pale skin, almost painfully beautiful. No wonder Bostridge had been embarrassed.

He was waiting for her to grab her clothes and leave while she could, like any other prostitute would have done, knowing the ropes, knowing that to stay around or get hysterical or look like anything other than a prostitute was to ask for a bullet. For whatever reason though, maybe just her youth, this one didn't know the ropes, and instead got down on the floor and ran her hand under the edge of the bed, as if looking for an earring or some other piece of lost jewelry.

He stared at her, transfixed, not sure at first whether she was in shock, oblivious to any danger, even to the fact that he was still there, watching, unable to take his eyes off her easy nakedness. He was hooked now anyway, wanting to know what she was looking for.

Finding nothing with her hand, she put the side of her face to the floor and looked underneath the bed, then got up and walked around to the other side. She seemed unhurried, completely unruffled by the death she'd just witnessed, a death that filled the room now with a visceral charge that was hard to ignore.

But Bostridge could have been sleeping it off for the complete disregard she was showing him as she moved around his corpse, as though she'd been in on the kill, as though she'd merely been biding her time in his grasp, waiting for the hitman so that she could get on with her part of the job. She hadn't been in on it though, and continued to ignore JJ too, like he didn't matter, like the two of them were in different dimensions, ghosts to each other.

This time she found what she was looking for, visible relief on her face as she pulled it from under the bed, something large and flat, a book or picture tied up in heavy cloth. She held it tight against her chest, lifted her clothes from one chair, her furs from another, shoes from the floor, never once easing her hold on it, clutching it against her breasts like she was suddenly trying to cover her nudity.

He wanted to see what was inside it but felt powerless to ask because of how absorbed she was, because of the air of total privacy that surrounded her. And in truth it had nothing to do with him anyway, and better to keep out of other people's business.

Finally she left, still without looking at him or at the man behind her on the bed. She looked content, or perhaps more, like she was trying to conceal her elation at having found the package. And despite the bewitching surface calm he could see now that her nerves were only just holding it together, that perhaps she did know how it was and wasn't convinced yet of making it out of there alive.

As she walked past him he drew in the stirred air, catching the smell of her perfume and a deeper musk that made him turn and stare after the last glimpse of her as she closed the door. The spell was broken then, leaving him alone with his work and a question mark over what could have been so important, what threat or promise had made her so determined that she would have that package.

Intrigued by association, he did a quick sweep on who Bostridge was, something he often did anyway if he had the time, for his own benefit, keeping ahead of the game. There wasn't much among the business cards and receipts though. His wallet contained a picture of him with his wife and two kids, an attractive family, part of the illusion.

Finally JJ came back to the man himself. What had he been doing there? JJ was guessing the package was art or religious plunder, so either he was a trader who did agency work on the side or he was an agency guy playing the black market. Either way, he'd somehow managed to take a hit from both lines of work in the same evening, JJ and the girl both sent there to do a job, both pulling it off smoothly.

Probably for a while there Bostridge had thought he was somebody; maybe that had been his problem, the way it was for a lot of Westerners doing business in Russia. And now he'd been reduced back to brutal truth, all pretense done with, transactions over, a flabby American with thinning hair, wearing only a yellow condom and a torn veil of blood across his face and chest.

When JJ left he found her sitting on one of the chairs facing the elevators, dressing slowly as though she'd been hit by fatigue, the package on the floor under the seat. She still looked beautiful in the harsher light out there, her skin flawless. He looked at her, hoping she'd glance up, but her eyes remained downcast as she worked through the thought-free movements of dressing.

He even turned to face her in the elevator before pressing to go down, staring at her again. She was buttoning her blouse, simple and white, expensive; not the kind of girl who got picked up on the street or in any old bar. Maybe Bostridge had been a family man after all, but whoever had sent this girl had chosen a bait he wouldn't have been able to resist.

She reached the top button as the doors began to close and for the first time she looked up, gray eyes fixing him with a gaze too expressive to read, of youth and premature wisdom and a plaintive yearning, something out of reach. Without thinking about it, his hand lifted and pressed the control panel, the doors stopping in their tracks and opening again.

They held each other's gaze for thirty seconds more. He wanted to speak to her, to say something, anything, but what was there to say? She was a teenage girl who'd just seen him kill a man, a girl he should have killed too but who'd captivated him because of the way she'd behaved and because he'd seen her naked and she was beautiful. There was no other bond between them, no other unspoken territories to explore. He let the doors close the second time, let her disappear, her eyes on him till the last.

He couldn't get her out of his thoughts though. In the cab on the way back to his own hotel he stared out of the window, a heavy sleet falling, lights and shadows from the passing traffic, and he kept seeing her face and the way she'd looked at him. And in the back of his mind he was telling the driver to turn around and calculating whether it was too late to catch her before she disappeared into the city darkness.

He knew he'd regret not doing it. There'd been something about her, something different, a secret locked away and communicated to him in code with that one acknowledgment of his presence. He knew if he didn't go back he'd be haunted by her. Even now he was regretting that he hadn't spoken, hadn't asked her name or where she lived, hadn't asked what was in the package, what could be so precious that she'd been willing to risk her life for it.

Whether or not, he remained silent, the driver continued on his way, the girl on hers. He wanted to go back, but it was easier not to. He closed his eyes, listening to the background hum of the engine, the rhythmic squeaking of the wipers, the surface water hissing under the tires. He switched off and let himself be lulled and thought of nothing. It was one of his weaknesses; sometimes he thought too much.

The weather had worsened the following day, an icy sleet driven horizontal by the wind. The plane sat on the tarmac for longer than expected, and when it finally began to taxi there was an uncomfortable silence. JJ was uneasy with the whole thing but bemused too that no one was saying out loud what they were all thinking: that it was crazy to take off in these conditions, that the plane would crash.

The silence became breathable as the plane built speed, as

the nose lifted, the stomach-tugging pull away from the ground. They were climbing steeply but it felt like they weren't going fast enough, and then for a moment the wind seemed to buffet them, knocking the plane to one side with a judder, throwing the engines into a sickening whine. Still the other passengers remained quiet, but he could feel them clenching their armrests just as hard as he was.

Within a few minutes it was all over. The plane continued climbing but less steeply, its course smoothened, the cabin slowly returning to the business of flying. People began to speak, conversation and laughter spilling out as they let off steam. The middle-aged guy next to him was polishing his glasses frantically and said in JJ's direction, "Makes you count your blessings, doesn't it?"

He smiled but didn't say anything. He wasn't sure what his blessings were—that he was a twenty-eight-year-old history graduate who'd somehow managed to end up killing people for a living, that he was alive himself for the time being, that in some small intangible way he was beginning to fall through the cracks. Maybe it would have been a blessing if the plane had crashed.

The guy finally put his glasses back on and said, "My wife won't fly at all; she was in a plane crash once." JJ turned to look at him, showing interest. "Oh, not a serious one. The plane overshot the runway into a field. Not a crash really, an incident, but one of the passengers was killed. Something fell from a luggage locker and hit him."

JJ nodded. "Some people die really easily."

"That's true. Yet some seem to survive almost anything."

He nodded again and let it drop, but that was true as well; some people did take a lot of killing.

Farther up the plane one of the flight attendants was

crouching talking to a passenger. He could hear her say, "The plane really wasn't in any danger." Her voice was familiar. When she stood and turned, smiling, he blanked for a second but then remembered where he knew her from. As she walked toward him he caught her eye. She smiled back, not recognizing him.

"Hello, Aurianne." Her smile faltered, looking puzzled at the edges. He laughed, adding, "We met skiing one weekend last winter."

She grinned at the explanation and said, "I don't believe it! JJ. I didn't recognize you."

"No. Different environment."

She looked, her eyes mischievous. "Why didn't we swap numbers?"

He shrugged his shoulders, and she answered herself, "I thought we were bound to run into each other in Geneva. It's strange how we haven't, isn't it?"

"Oh, I don't know. We both seem to travel a lot."

Someone called her farther down the aisle. Aurianne looked away, saying, "I'll be back." After she'd gone he could sense the guy next to him itching to say something, but JJ didn't turn, didn't give him license.

He was thinking about the weekend they'd met, how they'd hit it off, how they'd kissed late on the Saturday night but only kissed, a sure sign they'd expected to see more of each other. He couldn't remember why they hadn't. Possibly he'd taken for granted too that they would bump into each other again, or perhaps nine months before the need hadn't been strong enough.

It was a while before Aurianne got back to him, but she threw him knowing glances every time she passed. She was pretty. He liked her mouth and her eyes—dark laughing eyes, full of fun. He even liked the way she looked on duty, her hair pulled back, her uniform offering hints of what lay beneath.

When she eventually came back it was only to apologize for being so busy. Then she said, "Do you have plans for dinner tonight?"

"I feel I'm about to."

She grinned again. "Good. Speak to you later."

Still aware of the guy next to him, JJ leaned back in his seat and closed his eyes, not wanting to speak inanities.

He thought about the trip which, when it all stacked up, hadn't been that bad. There'd been a couple of inconveniences, the usual things around the periphery, but the job itself had gone smoothly, and now there was this, bumping into Aurianne. He'd still hassle Viner about the information though, partly for the hell of it but partly to keep him on his toes, because this time it had been a prostitute but the next it would be a bodyguard and then a whole militia.

Naked, he'd been gagged, had his feet bound and hands tied behind his back; that much he'd undoubtedly paid for. He'd probably paid for the knife too, something heavy-duty and symbolic, and they'd have been a good way into it before he'd realized he was getting more than he'd asked for, the subtle transition from client to victim.

At some point, as the bruising had bitten deeper and the blade had begun easing into flesh, he'd have known, and then some point later he'd have stopped whining and crying, begging through his gag, and then one or more times he'd have passed out, from the pain and eventually from the loss of blood. He'd been dead, or as good as, long before the final burst of violence had hacked through his neck.

So that was it for Viner. The collection of eighteenth-century furniture would be auctioned off, some of it after

restoration, and likewise his library. His other library would
be confiscated by the authorities, destroyed or mislaid. The
apartment would go on the market, but people would know
what had happened there so it would probably be another
foreigner who bought it. And at some stage in the cleaning
process someone else would come too and sweep the place,
mopping up any last fragments of his professional life. After
that, there'd be nothing.

The phone was by the windows which were open, so when JJ
sat down the pervasive smell in the room was held back a little by the street air. The body too was obscured by the furniture, but from where he sat he could see the raggedly
separated head lying on its side under a chair, eyes open,
staring, carpet-level toward the door where he'd come in.

It didn't look like a hit. Viner had gone in for rough with
street kids—a cheap explanation but probably close. It definitely didn't look like a hit; that was the only thing that mattered. He'd call London, sort out a new handler, and then
he'd be back to business as usual. It was a shame though,
Viner had been okay.

As okay as people got, anyway. His material could be as
off-target as anyone else's, and when it came down to the
wire he'd have sold people. But it had never come down to
the wire and for the most part he'd been sound, sick in the
sexual department but one of the few when it came to business.

A scooter tore up the street below; early evening, the city
quiet, a time for teenagers to tear up streets on scooters, the
whole night ahead, possibilities. It was a great time of day
out there in the city, disjointed sounds playing out the bot-

tom of the lull. He found himself distracted by it, drawn way into some indistinct memory, then pulled back again by the smell lapping toward him at the faltering of the breeze.

It made some people sick, the different ways death smelled, but it was a skill worth having, to be able to smell a corpse and know it. And the smell here wasn't the worst; Viner had soiled himself but he was still fresh, had probably been there only a few hours, an early-afternoon rendezvous turned sour.

JJ tapped out the numbers on the phone and waited, then let the alarm tone sink in and the automated telecom voice repeating itself. Please try again. He tapped them out again and listened, put the handset down and stared at it, puzzled. Numbers like that didn't change, didn't stop being available; it didn't make sense. He tapped it out a third time, carefully, more deliberately, got the same result, and put the phone down.

Another number reeled itself off in his head, but he held off using it. Something was badly wrong; for the contact number not to be working, there had to be a mess somewhere. He still couldn't quite believe the scene in front of him was wrapped up with it, but suddenly he was uncomfortable, no longer certain it was a good idea to get in touch.

It hardly seemed necessary, but he tapped out a random number to cover his tracks, putting the phone down as soon as it rang. It was reassuring somehow to imagine some early-evening apartment, thrown into a moment's suspended animation by that single ring of the phone, its occupants yanked by the leash and then released again to speculate on who might have called.

And the thought of another apartment made him look once more at Viner's. It was too tidy, a couple of things knocked around near the body but the rest of the place un-touched, or else turned over by someone who knew what he was doing. If a rent boy had done it he'd have ransacked the place. The way it looked just didn't square with the way the man had been killed.

JJ glanced back at the phone and then stared at the door, listening; quiet footsteps outside. He moved his hand inside his jacket but let it fall away again as whoever it was knocked tentatively. It was instinct, a sense that the person on the other side of that knock wouldn't know where to begin being a threat to him.

Things were getting interesting though. And it was like it was nothing to do with him, like he was just a spectator, cut off from the whole little drama by the stench rising off Viner's body. He was on the edge of it, more a part of evening in the city than a part of what was happening in front of him. Because of the telephone. The telephone had cut him loose, and as long as he spoke to no one he'd stay that way.

There was another knock, and a few seconds later the door opened, hesitantly, almost apologetically. Battered red Converse, that's what Viner would have seen from down there under his chair, and maybe that would have been enough to recognize him. He certainly had the look of one of Viner's boys—jeans, T-shirt, scruffy black hair, young face, lean.

The only thing that didn't fit was his nationality. He looked like a French kid, but as he bridled against the smell in the room he muttered some curse or other. An American. That was wrong. French and Arab boys JJ had seen there plenty of times but never American, and not just because of supply. It was a language thing; Viner had never liked sex with boys who spoke his own language.

The kid was carrying a sports bag and reached into it now, holding his breath, and pulled out what was inside. Then for the first time he saw JJ sitting there and stood frozen for a second, not breathing, his face straining at the building up of pressure.

A police siren sifted toward them, a few blocks away or even farther on calm streets, homing in on some accident or domestic somewhere. And the two of them stared at each other and then the American looked at the machete in his own hand and laughed, the breath bursting out of him. "Jesus, this must look weird, but then you must know about it, right? I was told to leave it here, or give it to you I guess."

"Not me. Him maybe."

The kid looked confused, then stared at the mess of furniture for a while before making out the body. The machete fell to the floor with a muffled clunk. The police siren hovered in the middle distance, apparently going nowhere. The kid had doubled over and looked set to empty his stomach.

JJ jumped out of the chair toward him. "Don't be sick. Stand up." He lifted the kid by the shoulders so they were face-to-face, the kid's suddenly like a drunk's, pasty and unfocused. "Don't be sick, okay? Control it, just control it. Breathe." He nodded like he understood, made a conscious effort to get his lungs working. "Did you know Viner?" He shook his head, still fighting the need to vomit. Now that JJ looked at him, he could see the kid was older, nineteen or twenty, much too old to have been one of Viner's boys. "Have you been here before?"

Again, no, and this time he spoke, his voice high and shaky. "Two guys paid me a thousand francs to deliver the blade, no questions asked. They gave me the address, told me what to do."

"What were they like? The two guys, what were they like?"

He was shaking his head as if to everything. "I don't know. They were just . . . they were your guys, you know."

"What do you mean, mine?"

"They were British. You're English, right?"

Like his ears were stacking it up for him, JJ became aware of the siren again. It had jumped closer, much closer, turning the corner maybe, the end of the street. "You've been set up! Get the machete and the bag—follow me."

"What? What's happening?" The kid was still dazed, but he too could hear the siren now, his eyes darting to the windows and back.

"Do you want to end up like him?" JJ pointed at the naked body, lacerated and stained. "Then get the machete and the bag and follow me." This time the American moved, urgency taking him over, and with the siren's wail increasingly smothered, JJ was leading him out the back way and through the broken pathways he'd mapped a few years before, an escape route, one which would give him some distance in the event of something like this happening.

Not that he knew what had happened. The kid quickly getting out of breath behind him, his lungs beginning to rasp like they were bleeding, he was the one who'd been set up. JJ had just stumbled in there by mistake. But he'd stumbled in on something; it was just a question of finding out how big and how he stood in the middle of it.

For one thing, Viner had clearly been hit after all, and dressed up like voodoo for whatever reason. They'd set the kid up, British guys, probably arranged it with the police. And then there was that failed number. If the two were connected it was about as big as things could get. If they were connected then perhaps JJ really was cut loose.

They were descending flights of stairs, their steps producing no noise, the American's painful breathing grating through
the quiet though, and the sports bag finding obstacles in the
walls and banisters. The police siren was gone, silence in the
building around them, no televisions, no arguments, nothing
to suggest they were passing through people's lives.

And a few minutes later they were in a back courtyard,
darkness already falling among the surrounding walls, the
visible street empty. JJ stood looking at the kid, bent double
again, coughing up heavy phlegm, drooling. They hadn't run
hard or far, so either he was ill or it was nerves.

Then perhaps he had a right to be nervous. Fifteen minutes before he'd probably felt like the luckiest loser in town,
money in his pocket for running some mindless errand, and
now he was just scared of dying too soon or being locked up
or even hurt. JJ would have been scared too at that age. Not
anymore though; at some point in the years between he'd
had most of his nerves nickel-plated.

They were tingling now but for all the wrong reasons. It
was the thought of what must have happened. If London
had shut down the channels there must have been a mother
security breach, and if Viner being killed was part of it then
there was some sort of purge or turf war going on. It was
that possibility that excited him. He wasn't sure why but the
idea of the system suddenly spinning out of control appealed
to him.

The American had recovered enough to stop coughing,
but he was still leaning over, hands on knees, muttering
curses. JJ wasn't certain why he'd brought him. He'd been
caught in the middle of some other train of thought and had
wanted to help the kid out of a fix. Possibly, given longer to
think, he'd have left him there.

As it was, he supposed he could give him a few thousand

francs, tell him to lose the weapon, get out of Paris. He had
the look about him anyway of someone who just wanted to
get out of Paris, out of Europe, back home to wherever it
was he'd wanted to escape from in the first place. There was
no real risk of him talking.

It crossed JJ's mind to ask again about the men who'd
paid him, but even if the kid knew anything, it was hardly information JJ could use. And if things had shut down it
would be only temporary; it wasn't like he'd be out of business for good. For all his flights of fancy, the chances were
within a few days everything would be back to normal. The
only thing he needed to know for sure was that it was actually happening. After that it was just a question of keeping
out of the way till things had calmed down.

Collecting his thoughts, JJ pulled his gun and shot the kid
twice, first through the side of the ribs, then in the head just
above the ear, the second shot after he'd slumped to the
ground. He went quietly, still drooling, and thinking about it
JJ didn't know why he'd ever considered any other option.
After all, what kind of person took money from strangers? A
desperate person maybe, a kid, still not somebody he wanted
walking the streets with an imprint of his face.

The kid looked quite graceful now on the hard stone floor,
like the kill in a hunt, like a leopard or cheetah. It didn't matter how pathetic or otherwise his life had been, he was beautiful now, composed. And within a few days he'd probably
make the papers and move people here and there in the sub-
urbs of America, and it would seem quite exotic, that he had
gone to Paris and been killed there.

3

JJ walked back to the hotel, the city's metabolism building and night creeping up from the pavements, darkness wrapping itself around the people and cars on the streets, shards of noise and light, expectation mounting.

They were tourists mainly, entwined couples separating for no one, middle-aged ones clutching their bags and camcorders, all of them locked into their own personal highs. The Parisians were easy to identify; they were the ones who saw him, who made fleeting eye contact in the seconds they took to pass.

And none of them would remember his face. That was what he liked about city streets; there was no remembering the faces. He could walk like a wraith between worlds and be untouched by both of them. It was good too that those worlds rarely crossed into each other, that the pedestrians flowing around him would never know and never need to know why someone called Viner was dead.

That was only on the streets though. In the hotel he could feel himself slipping back into it, the corridors desolate except for a baby crying somewhere in one of the rooms, a stealthy silence draped over the functional sounds of the building. It was places and times like this that Viner was dead, out on the blank edges of other people's daily existence.

The room said it too, oppressively calm, desperate, suffocating, like it was wrong to be there at that time of the evening. He sat on the bed, phoned room service to order something to eat, but changed his mind, the woman at the other end barely masking her irritation. He checked his watch, thinking it better to get the lowdown from Danny and then move on straight away.

He dialed and as soon as the answering machine clicked in said, "It's JJ, pick up." For a few seconds the message continued before Danny lifted the phone, at first competing with his own recorded voice. "Hey, JJ, it's good to hear from you. I suppose you wanna know what's happening?"

"Something like that. I'm in Paris."

That threw him for a second, his reply cautious. "On business?"

"No, a private matter, but I took the opportunity of visiting an old friend, and I have to say, he wasn't looking too good."

Danny sighed and said, "Yeah. I had some traffic that Viner was down. You have to admit though, he would have been whacked anyway sooner or later."

JJ smiled at the terminology, Danny's fixation on the Mob.

"It's not just Viner though, is it?" He was guessing, but Danny always gave more to people who sounded informed in

the first place. He still responded as if to a massive under-
statement.

"No, no, no." There was a pause. He was eating, his voice
like cotton wool when he spoke again. "You're just about the
only one of Viner's people left. I'm hearing Townsend's
down, so is Hooper. Berg's down, of all people. Only person
ahead of the game looks like Lo Bello. Him and his people
have been bermuda since last Friday—not a trace."

"That doesn't surprise me—Lo Bello's a shrewd operator." But so were some of the other names he'd reeled off.
"What about Berg's people?"

Danny laughed, saying, "The beautiful Esther's gone to
ground if that's what you're wondering, but of the immediate crew the only other one still unaccounted for is David
Philips. Exciting stuff, isn't it?"

JJ didn't acknowledge the question, but he could feel
small surges of adrenaline firing off in his bloodstream.
"Who is it?"

"Well as to who's doing all the killing, your guess is as
good as mine. London's just found out it's been in bed with
the Russian Mafia for the last four or five years—something
I think *we* could have guessed four or five years ago. So I'd
say London's overreacting, the Russians have panicked and
started closing people down themselves, and our friends in
Arlington have probably joined in because they've got nothing better to do. There's just a real meltdown going on out
there. It's crazy; they're gonna regret some of the people
they've hit in the last couple of days."

"Not half as much as the people they've hit."

"Yeah, but stiffs don't vote."

"Not as a rule. What about me, Danny?"

Another mouthful of food. "Obviously, it doesn't make

sense for anyone to take you out, but that doesn't mean you're not on a list. I'd say the big thing in your favor is your, er, contractual status—you're not as easy to track. If you were an employee and they wanted you dead, you'd be dead by now."

"So it seems."

"Too true. So play your advantage, disappear for a week or so till it's blown over. Once they're all thinking straight you'll be okay. I mean, you whack the pimps, not the hookers."

JJ smiled and said, "You seem pretty relaxed."

"Please, JJ, a retired pimp isn't worth the price of a bullet."

"Nor the airfare to Sweden."

Danny laughed, saying, "Exactly. So anyway, go on holiday, relax, call me in a week, ten days, and I'll let you know the score."

"Sure."

"Oh, and it should go without saying, but don't go back to Geneva."

"So I'm gonna have to buy new beach clothes?"

Danny came back at him confidently. "You can afford it. And in a few weeks I'd say you'll be able to renegotiate your fee."

"An interesting thought. Speak to you soon, Danny."

"Hey, I'll be here."

JJ put the phone down and checked his watch. Then he thought of Aurianne and immediately felt his stomach turn as what Danny had said hit home: don't go back to Geneva. They'd know about her, had to know about her by now.

He picked the phone up again and dialed, smiling at first when the machine clicked in at the other end. She was ill at ease with her answering machine, one of those people who tried too hard to make her voice sound relaxed, the result, if anything, ending up strangely stilted. Slowly though he found the smile straightening out, the awkwardly voiced message he'd heard so many times before suddenly troubling him. He didn't want to speak but did anyway. "It's me. I have to go away for a couple of weeks. Don't call. Don't come round to my place. Don't even leave a message. I'll call you as soon as I get back."

It was wasted. He could feel it in his gut, a creeping nausea; she was already dead. He kept trying to dismiss it, but it was there like a certainty. Like Danny had said, there was a meltdown in progress and it had taken Aurianne with it, just like it had taken Viner, like it had taken the kid in the alley. It didn't make sense that anyone would choose to kill her. But that was exactly what happened at times like this, innocent people got killed.

He looked at the room, too small, a hotel he wouldn't use again. And he tried to piece together what he was thinking because a part of him was still clinging stubbornly to the idea that she was alive, that she was simply out or sleeping. He phoned again from the station for the same reason, let the message run its course, ignoring the cold logic of it with the thought that if he wasn't a target she wouldn't be one by association.

But he was a target. Someone had been sent to Geneva just as surely as someone had been sent to Paris for Viner. They'd failed to find him though, so they'd gone to Aurianne's, had no doubt tried to get something out of her before killing her. They'd still be there somewhere, in her apartment or his, waiting on station but no longer believing he'd show, particularly now, the contents of his call to Danny already distilled and drip-fed back to them.

Once he was on the train he thought again about what Danny had said, but there was no choice, he had to know for sure. And he'd have the element of surprise on his side. The train would get him there first thing, and he'd be out on an early flight before they even realized he'd been there. He'd take her with him if she was okay, but with the night drawing on that thought was already failing in his mind, becoming just a token response to an unpalatable truth.

He stared at the window, a softly lit version of the car reflected against the night, his own face visible from the corner of his eye. There were only a handful of other people reflected there: an elderly woman reading, the rest traveling students: two girls sleeping, a small group talking at the far end, a guy on his own looking bored.

JJ wished he could be like them, wished he could just be a person traveling, no mental baggage, of no interest to anyone else. Some of them probably felt the same way, he was aware of that. He resented it though, resented that he was in so deep and that, despite what Danny had said, it was never just a question of disappearing for a while. He was tied in too tight.

4

Her apartment was empty, none of the choked-up early-morning airlessness of places which had been occupied and slept in. It was clean too, no coffee cups, no makeshift ashtrays, no leftover take-out cartons. It looked pale and pure, the way she'd planned it, the climbing sun blurring the edges of her minimalist living room, the fine spray of blood almost lost in the luminous white of the carpet, only the smudged red patch easily visible, where she'd fallen, where her head had temporarily rested. She'd been kneeling.

The bedroom was untidy, the look of morning but without the feel of it, missing the scent markers of a person only briefly absent, in the shower or making coffee in the kitchen. She'd been out of bed maybe thirty minutes when they'd come, probably the previous morning, her routine interrupted and left now like an exhibit, like something from Pompeii.

He checked the bathroom, strolled back out, and caught

his first glimpse of the kitchen. It took him a moment to work out what was on the floor. At first it looked like the debris of a scuffle, but then he saw it for what it was—the shelves from the fridge, pulled out and thrown aside.

He walked toward it, and though he'd known she was dead he could feel the contents of his chest sinking at the sight of the shelves, the realization that he was finally about to be confronted by it, all doubt removed. He pulled the door open and stared, nodding gently at the cauterizing truth of it and at the strange completeness of seeing her there.

It was a big fridge and Aurianne was slim and lithe, but she looked uncomfortable even in death the way she'd been bundled fetal position into its white plastic confines. With the door open the light illuminated the side of her face, bruised around the mouth and in a line from her eye to her ear. The eye was swollen shut, the ear filled with congealed blood, and more blood matted her hair, enough for him to see the blows as they'd fallen. The bullet itself had gone in the other side and hadn't come through.

He looked at her cramped body, not bruised but blood spattered. She was naked, had probably been raped as part of the process and, ironically, wouldn't have been able to talk because she'd known almost nothing about him. The guy would have known that too, whoever he was, but some people got their kicks that way, under the guise of ruthlessness and efficiency.

He reached out to touch her but drew back reflexively from the cold air. He hadn't been in love with her. He'd loved who she was, and they'd been happy together but they hadn't been in love. That made it worse, because he wanted to feel grief but felt guilt instead, and a disjointed sadness, even relief. But no real grief.

He pushed the door closed, the rubber seal kissing shut, and he stared vacantly for a few seconds, searching for feelings that wouldn't come. Eventually, a different line of thought rose up to fill the emptiness, and he thought ahead and thought of Athens. He had a box there. If he was flying out then Athens was the best place to make for. He could stay there a week or so before it became too risky, maybe longer if he had to. And if he did have to move on, it was a good place to move on from. He'd go to Athens that morning, as soon as he'd finished what he had left to do.

He walked back into the bedroom before he left, for one last look, taking it all in, the crumpled, lived-in quality that had always been missing from the living room, the memory of her sitting there on the bed, reading, drinking coffee. It was easier to conjure up her presence there than anywhere else.

He sat on the edge of the mattress, the duvet thrown back, and smoothed his hand over the sheet she'd slept on. He picked up the pillow then and held it to his face, breathing in the faint smell of her that remained there, his memory almost overwhelmed by it, by everything it brought to mind.

And then he stood and made to walk out but still turned and looked again. It never ceased to cause him wonder, that here had been a living person and now she was gone, fading away again, the city waking up without her as if she'd never been there. It was an incredible thing, beyond comprehension, as incredible as being there in the first place.

He emerged from the building, the air reviving him. With the sun not on it yet the street was cold and fresh. The taxi driver was still there, like he'd had nowhere to go at that time of the morning, driver door open, one foot resting on the pavement. He was drinking coffee, the flask on the passenger seat, steam creeping up off the cup and out of the car.

He was surprised to see JJ again but made a gesture as if to say he'd finish the drink quickly.

"No, take your time. I'm in no hurry." JJ got in the back and looked at the building across the street, top half sunlit, the bottom looking like an early taste of winter. It occurred to him that he'd probably never see that street again in winter, that he'd never been to that part of town before he'd met her and would probably never go there again. For some reason it made him sad, sadder even than the thought of never seeing Aurianne again, never seeing her smile, never hearing her speak in English.

The driver seemed nervous with him just sitting in the back like that, silent, eyes on the street, and he finished his coffee quickly anyway, wiping the cup dry with a paper napkin before putting it back on the flask. He closed the door and started the engine and looked in the rearview mirror, eye contact once removed, saying he was ready, but only if his passenger was ready.

JJ responded with a token smile and nodded for him to drive on, giving him general directions at first, then closing in, more specific. When they got there he had him pull up right outside, not down the street like a lot of people would have done. And this time he told him to wait, fifteen minutes or so, told him even that they'd be going to the airport.

He moved quickly through the lobby and up the stairs, opened the lock, let the door slip ajar an inch, and waited, listening. He could hear someone in the kitchen and knew automatically from the time of day what was happening. There were two of them, one sleeping. He couldn't help but think of Aurianne's body being eased into her fridge. But this was different; the owner of this apartment was still alive.

He stepped inside and waited against the wall. He could see the door to his bedroom closed and a loaded holster sitting on the low table in the living room, looking like a chic black handbag from that angle. Whoever was in the kitchen deserved a slap for having left it there, but it was the kind of lapse of judgment most people fell into sooner or later.

He came out then, a guy about JJ's own age or younger, no one he knew, wearing a plain shirt, dark trousers. JJ glanced back at the living room and saw a tie draped over one arm of the chair he'd been sitting on. He was carrying a tray with a pot of coffee and a cup on it, and he was laughing to himself, maybe about how domesticated it all seemed. He shifted the tray into one hand as he got to the bedroom, knocked on the door, got some response, and started to open it.

It had to be now. JJ vaulted off the wall and threw his weight into the square of the other guy's back, slamming him into the room, a crash of body, tray, coffeepot, cup. Without even getting a look at him, he took out the guy on the bed with one shot, still startled and bleary-eyed and a good few heartbeats away from thinking of going for his gun. It was Ian Wilson, someone he'd met a couple of times and knew something about.

The younger guy was thrashing around like a fish on deck, scalded by the coffee where it had gone through his shirt, his bearings scattered. He instinctively went for his holster, found it missing, seemed to come back to himself, and suddenly became calm, sitting up where he'd fallen on the floor. He stared at Wilson's body twitching on the bed, then looked up.

"There's a chair behind you. Why don't you shuffle backwards and put yourself in it?"

The guy moved slowly, eyes dulled in submission. Once he was sitting JJ said, "Do you know anything about me?"

He tried to speak, found his voice constricted, and cleared his throat before trying again. "Not officially. Stuff he told me."

"So you know that if I wanted to kill you, you'd be dead by now." He nodded, noncommittal. "So relax, you're okay. I just need one piece of information and once I've got it I'll have no reason to kill you. In fact, you can take a message back for me."

"What piece of information?"

"Who sent you?"

The guy made an attempt at looking puzzled and said, "London. I don't know who. I don't think Wilson knew."

"How old are you?"

"What?"

"Who has the gun here? Just answer the question."

"Twenty-nine."

"But you're new in." He nodded. "So I'm guessing you were in the services before. British Army?" He didn't nod this time but the guess was correct, the haircut as much a giveaway as anything else. "And it was you who interrogated my girlfriend."

"Wilson killed her."

"But you interrogated her. And now that I know this piece of shit was involved I know for sure you raped her too." He was shaking his head, his face playing nervous games. "He'd have pushed you if you needed it, cajoled you into it, told you how good it was at breaking them down, but he'd have got you to do it because he always got off on watching it. Or didn't you know that?"

"You're mistaken. I . . . look, I . . ."

"Don't lie to me. I know she was raped and I know it was you who did it."

His face was pleading, on the verge of breaking down, his head moving nervously from side to side. It didn't seem so much that he was scared, more that he knew it had been wrong and was regretting it now, regretting that he'd allowed himself to be swept into it, that he'd allowed his professionalism to be teased away from him by someone like Wilson. "It was just . . . I didn't know."

JJ cut him short, his voice still calm though. "You didn't know? Do you know what city you're in? You raped her. That's what you did, you raped her, so what I'm gonna do now is graze one of these bullets off your balls and when you come round I'm gonna do it again and keep doing it until you tell me who sent you." JJ aimed the gun between his legs.

"Berg sent us."

"Berg's dead." He fired, putting a hole in the seat of the chair. The guy let out a hollow wail, like all the air being sucked out of his lungs, and slumped, his head lolling to the side, the crotch of his trousers suddenly torn and bloody where the bullet had gone through.

Either Berg was dead or even Danny didn't know what was going on. JJ got a bag from the bottom of the closet and started choosing clothes to go in it. And all the while he was thinking through the time scale, when it must have started, whether Berg could have ordered his hit before being hit himself. He couldn't even think why Berg would have had any reason to hit him, so maybe it had been someone higher or not Berg at all but someone lower, someone like Wilson playing loose.

He'd almost finished packing when the guy in the chair moaned as he began to come around. JJ looked over, watched the guy's head slowly lifting, then took his gun again and shot him from across the room, a clean finish. He looked at the two of them, one on the bed, one in the chair. The room would have to be redecorated, but maybe they'd deal with that when they came to remove the bodies. He didn't know what the procedure was, but there was bound to be some department that dealt with it.

He was idly thinking about it when the phone rang, loud and shrill against the silence of the apartment and the early morning. He weighed for a second whether or not he should answer it, then walked into the living room and picked it up, reckoning it was his phone and he was there so what difference did it make?

"Hello?"

There was a pause at the other end, like the caller hadn't expected an answer. Then an American accent came back at him, middle-aged, gravelly around the edges. "Could I speak to David Bostridge please?"

JJ took a second to place the name, Bostridge, the guy he'd hit a couple of years ago in Moscow, an intriguing choice in itself. "Only if you know a good medium," he said, and the American seemed to sigh with relief before replying, "Thank God. You don't know me, Mr. Hoffman. My name's Ed Holden. I have some important information for you."

"Go on."

"Whatever you think is going on at the moment, you're wrong. Someone wants you dead." As an information source he seemed a little after the fact.

"So I gather," said JJ flippantly.

The American came back at him, hesitant but determined to make a distinction. "No, you don't. This isn't panic, this isn't the fallout of something else. Someone wants *you* dead, you specifically, just like they want me dead. There's no sitting this one out. You and I, we're both marked."

JJ didn't know who he was, but he sounded like someone

who knew his time was up, clutching at anything that might save him, hoping to convince someone like JJ to come in on his own protection. It was definitely intriguing though, how he knew about him in the first place, how he knew about the Bostridge hit, why he'd chosen it as an identifying device.

"Okay, Holden," said JJ, businesslike but relaxed, "how about some meat on these bones? Who are you, who do you work for, why the concern for my welfare?"

The reply was determined again. "It doesn't matter who I am. I called you because you can help me stay alive and I have the information you need to do the same." His tone shifted, becoming instructional. "Now, I'm on the move and I'll be secure by tomorrow morning our time. You have an American friend in London. Tell him I've gone to ground and there's nowhere to swim. He'll know where I am."

He was talking about Tom Furst, a CIA contact JJ hadn't spoken to in a year. So maybe that explained who Holden was too, and the way things looked at the moment he was probably safer playing with the CIA than anyone else, but the way things looked at the moment that probably didn't count for much either. And if this was too devious or too flaky to be a trap, it still had a smell about it, the smell of someone knowing too much about him.

He thought of Danny urging him to treat it like a holiday, being right too about not coming back to Geneva. The previous afternoon he hadn't felt like he needed a holiday, but it was tempting now, the urge to escape everything he was having to deal with all of a sudden, the intrigue not enough of a lure on its own to hold him back; if he'd wanted intrigue he'd have become a spy.

"I'm sorry, Holden. You may well be right, but I'd rather take the odds. And speaking of which, they're getting shorter every minute I stay on the phone." There was another pause before Holden answered. JJ finally realized they weren't pauses at all but the satellite delay, and when Holden spoke he sounded calm, confident.

"I understand your caution, Mr. Hoffman. But I can assure you, your chances of surviving without my help are negligible."

JJ felt insulted somehow, like Holden had slighted his abilities, abilities he didn't necessarily think came to much but that he felt the need to defend anyway, particularly with two bodies in his bedroom. "Perhaps you underestimate me. The fact I'm taking this call—"

Holden cut in abruptly, the interruption arriving a few words after he'd made it. "No, I know exactly how good you are. Perhaps you underestimate me, and what you're up against." It was a piece of bait JJ couldn't resist: to find out who this person was who was trying to kill him. Him specifically.

"And what am I up against? Who is it?"

"It's Berg." A tinny electronic echo bounced around in the earpiece: Berg.

Taken aback, JJ produced a knee-jerk derisive laugh and repeated himself from a few minutes before. "Berg's dead. And even if he wasn't, why would he want me dead?"

But he had no choice now other than to start believing. Two people pointing a finger in the same direction was too much of a coincidence. So maybe Berg was still alive, and maybe the purge Danny had talked about was just a cover for something smaller, more personal. He still couldn't think though why Berg would want him dead, and as if to back up that doubt Holden answered cagily, "I'm still piecing that together. Believe me though, Berg's alive."

Possibly he was, but there was nothing more JJ could say, and conscious suddenly of how long he'd been on the phone and of the taxi waiting outside, conscious too of giving his thoughts away, he said, "Okay, I have to go. I need to think this over for a few days. Then I'll decide what to do."

There was the pause again, seeming significant but meaning nothing, before Holden replied, "I hope you have a few days."

"Thanks for your concern. Maybe I'll be in touch." He put the phone down and without stopping to think got the bag from the bedroom and headed down to the taxi.

It was only as they made for the airport that he began raking over things again, Aurianne mainly, the confusion and mystery about who was trying to kill whom feeling obscene and petty against the unfairness of what had happened to her.

It wasn't just her either, because however shallow things had been between them, they'd been happy together. And for two years he'd started to believe he could lead a life separate from what he did. They'd been two people whose jobs had taken them away a lot, that was all, and when they'd been together they'd been like any other young couple, almost, a life that was stable, something that had felt like normality.

But now here he was heading away from it, feeling like those two years had never happened, feeling naïve and stupid for never having seen reality sitting out there on the horizon, waiting to make its move. He should have known better too, from the number of lives upon which he'd visited that same brand of shock therapy realism.

Approaching the airport he came around to the present again, realizing he still hadn't decided what to do. He felt he needed the couple of weeks lying low that Danny had suggested, felt like he needed to lie somewhere with the late-summer sun working his skin, the heat of the Mediterranean.

But he'd already gone against what Danny had said, had gone back to Geneva and his apartment, and he'd been there to take that call from Holden, a one in a million chance. And if what Holden had said was true, maybe he didn't have those couple of weeks.

For a short while in Paris he'd felt a rush at the thought of what was happening, the real nature of it sinking in only now—that his life was falling apart. He'd been slowly heading toward certainty for two years, but now it was all gone, even in his professional life, no Viner to call and harangue, Danny looking crippled with misinformation, no one he knew he could trust.

He was reduced to guessing games, trying to guess what Holden was playing at, why a total stranger was offering to help him, trying to guess whether it really was Berg who wanted him bagged and tagged, trying to guess why. It was all about information, information at a level he didn't normally deal with, his usual way of quantifying threats based on bullets hitting the woodwork, on immediate risk, not on personalities and agendas.

Berg. JJ didn't even know him that well, familiar only with the unassuming exterior, knowing of no dangerous side. They'd never worked together either, so why would Berg have wanted to do this to him? Perhaps it wasn't Berg after all, and Danny was closer to the truth than JJ gave him credit for, but he had to find out. And Holden had gotten one thing right if nothing else: someone was undoubtedly trying to kill him. It was just a question of who, and how serious they were about it.

5

"Furst."

"Hello, Tom, it's JJ."

A fleeting moment of mental placing and Tom said, "Jesus, JJ. Where are you?"

"In London."

"So no one's after you either?"

He noted that final *either* but let it go for now and answered straight. "Oh, people are after me. Can we meet?"

"Of course. Come over."

"Stupid enough to be in London, Tom, not stupid enough to come skipping across Grosvenor Square." Tom laughed and JJ added, "If you come up North Audley there's a Waterstone's bookshop."

"I know it."

"Meet me in there in about fifteen minutes. I'll be looking through the thrillers."

"Where else? See you there."

JJ put the phone down and walked along the final fifty yards to the bookshop, the street brimming with people walking slowly, the air fume-sodden but warm and comfortable, like summer was getting a foothold rather than fading out.

In the bookstore he wandered around for a bit, checking where the exits were, making a quick survey of the handful of people browsing. He went over to a large table display of thrillers then and picked one up, pretending to read it while keeping an eye on the two ways Tom might come toward him.

When he noticed him approaching the main doors though, he lowered his eyes to the text and kept them there, sending out the message that there was no question of him not trusting the American. And only as Tom got close did JJ look up, smiling genuinely at the sight of him, the fresh preppy face, neat hair, the East Coast casual clothes.

"See anything you like?"

JJ shook his hand and said, "I'm looking at last pages."

Tom picked a book up too, idly flicked through it. "I've read a lot of these," he said. "They all try to be different, but the good guys usually live, bad guys usually die."

"It's knowing who's who is the problem."

"Oh, that's easy." Tom smiled, looking pleased with himself. "If you die you're bad, if you live you must be good—it's the cat in the box thing."

JJ nodded appreciatively and said, "Quantum physics, I like it." He paused then and added, "So anyway, do you have any idea what's going on?"

Tom frowned slightly, like they really had started talking quantum physics. "We're in the dark," he said, suddenly speaking as an organization. "We know something's going on, but we're basically in the position of sitting on our hands and watching it unfold." A blue pinstripe approached and started leafing through the array of thrillers. Tom looked around and said, "There's a café in here, isn't there?"

"Upstairs." JJ led the way, again making a point of being unguarded, of letting Tom out of his sight line.

The café was crowded, a lunchtime crowd, office and shop workers on their own or in pairs, more noise coming from the service and kitchen area than was coming from the room itself. They found a small table over to one side which hadn't been cleared. Tom moved the empty glass and a plate with remnants of a salad and baked potato on it. "You hungry?"

JJ shook his head.

"I'll get the coffee then. No, you don't drink coffee. Mint tea or lemon or something like that, right?"

"Yeah, whatever they have." He watched as Tom went over and got a tray and stood in the line, still something of the Ivy League student about him, a lightness of mood that gave nothing away of the information swimming around inside his head.

When he got to the head of the line he said something to tease the surly woman behind the counter into a smile, and kept at the banter while she loaded the tray with cups and pots of hot water and so on, leaving her with a glow, bashful and flattered. It was the way he was. Middle-aged women probably would have thrown themselves in the path of bullets to protect Tom Furst, JJ uncertain only as to whether he'd have let them.

He came back smiling and sat down, unloading the tray as he spoke. "Peppermint for you."

"Thanks."

"So, you didn't come into the lion's den for chitchat and wordplay. What can I do for you, JJ?"

"I had a call from someone called Ed Holden. He seems to

think you might know him." Tom looked impressed, either by
the name or by the fact that Holden had referred JJ to him.

"Known him since I was a kid," he said, "friend of my
dad's; they worked together in Berlin. He's an art history
professor at Yale now, officially retired years back but, you
know, he's been active in one capacity or another. Very well
connected."

The final words were weighted with meaning, but if he
was so well connected JJ wondered why he wasn't using
those connections rather than enlisting the help of a
stranger, unless of course he no longer trusted them, or unless JJ unwittingly had more to offer. He didn't think for a
moment there was any altruism involved. "Well this friend of
yours thinks the same person's trying to kill him and me. He
says this present business is cover for a settling of scores."

Tom nodded thoughtfully and sipped at his coffee,
spurring JJ to try the tea, the peppermint vapor almost overpowering.

"He could be onto something there. Some of the people
being taken down are minor players. I mean, some of them
don't even register. So it could be smoke and mirrors to cover
something else."

"What though?"

"Beats me." Tom looked around then before adding in a
lower voice, "Did Ed tell you who he thought wanted you
dead?"

"Philip Berg."

That was met with raised eyebrows, another sip of coffee,
Tom thinking it over before he replied. "I heard he was killed
two days ago. Not that what I heard means very much. And
it wouldn't be without precedent."

"What do you mean?"

Tom looked around again. JJ was amused by the way it

looked, like they were discussing some kind of office gossip—where the next demotion was coming, who was sleeping with whom.

"Berg was involved in a joint operation in the Middle East in the late eighties. It went wrong—spectacularly wrong if you know what I mean—and Berg was in it up to his neck. Then people started to have accidents, couple of people got taken down conventionally. This was before my time, but apparently we were pretty certain Berg was responsible. London was having none of it though, so it was allowed to drop. But within a year there was no one left who could point the finger at Berg."

JJ knew Berg had been in the Middle East, but it was the first time he'd heard anything like that about him, the man recast now as someone who looked after his people. Maybe the only unusual thing in retrospect was that Viner had never really spoken about him, perhaps knowing where it was best for his indiscretions to end. As of the previous afternoon though, discretion had stopped being enough.

"I think Berg's alive," JJ said, telling himself as much as Tom. "Even with what you've just told me though, one part of the equation doesn't fit."

"And what's that?"

"I've never worked for him, never crossed his path. I don't even really know anything about him."

"As far as you're aware, but clearly Ed thinks otherwise. Doesn't anything spring to mind?"

He shook his head but thought of the Bostridge job, a hit which as far as he knew had come through the normal channels. Yet Holden had used it as a way of checking who he was on the phone, which meant that he knew the details, and maybe that the connection was there too.

Reminding himself again that Holden's agenda was as much a mystery to him as Berg's, he said, "I know he's your friend, Tom, but what about me? Can I trust this guy Holden?"

"Definitely," he said without hesitation, backing it up then. "He's one of us, you know, whatever we are." JJ liked the touch of unquestioning inclusiveness, based on only rapport and a couple of favors exchanged. Tom's opinion was probably skewed anyway; Holden was a senior family friend he obviously revered, JJ merely a contact he valued, maybe respected.

"He told me you'd know where I could find him, that he'd gone to ground and there was nowhere to swim."

Tom smiled at the riddle. "The Copley Inn," he said immediately, "a guesthouse in Vermont, family friends."

"Do you have the number?"

"Not on me but we're in the right place to find it. There's a book of New England inns; it's in there. It's a great place by the way. You could get a flight to Boston . . ."

"No, I'll have to go in through New York, pick some things up. I'll take the train from there maybe, hire a car."

"The perfect cover," Tom said, laughing. "An English tourist in Vermont, September. You'll fit right in." He was obviously amused by the thought of JJ going there, like the two things didn't fit together in his mind.

"I can't wait," said JJ, humoring him. "Shall we find the travel section?"

Tom nodded and stood, looking at the table, and then like he'd remembered something important he walked over to the counter and put some change in the tip jar, exchanging a few more words with the woman there.

There was only one other person browsing in the travel

section, a girl who looked like she'd just come back from India, all batik and bangles and henna. Tom searched for a
while before saying, "We're in luck," pulling a slim glossy
paperback from the shelf. He leafed through the pages before
handing the open book to JJ, pointing with his other hand.
"There it is, the Copley Inn."

He looked at the color picture, taken in the autumn, a
large white clapboard house, an image familiar enough to
seem artificially picturesque. He looked at the text below but
stopped immediately at the name of the proprietor, alarm
bells ringing.

Without looking up he said, "Mrs. Susan Bostridge." Just
saying the name gave him a small kick of adrenaline.

"Yeah, her husband and Ed were business partners,
friends from way back, at Dartmouth together. Bostridge
was killed a couple of years ago."

"In Moscow, I know." JJ closed the book and looked at
Tom. "I don't know what Holden's playing at, but I can't go
there."

"Why not?"

"Because I've never met the family of a hit before and I
don't intend to start now. It's baggage I can do without."

Tom stared at him, taking a few seconds to work out what
JJ was getting at.

"You killed David Bostridge?" he said finally. "We thought
the Russians did it."

"That's how it was meant to look. I'm still surprised you
didn't know."

"Well, we didn't. Beats me why not."

JJ said, "Holden knows, and he knows I did it too. And
now it turns out he wants me to go to the house of his life-
long friend and business partner." It seemed obvious now,

the explanation for this stranger calling out of nowhere, perhaps aiming to settle his own score during the wider crisis.

"No, hold up," Tom said, looking concerned, eager to iron things out. "You're forgetting something. Ed's been in the business a long time; he knows you're just a gun. It's not his style."

"You can hardly blame me for being suspicious."

"Maybe not. But I'll tell you something, JJ, if he says Berg wants you dead, believe him, and if he says he can help you—well believe that too. I mean, I can understand you not wanting to go there, for lots of reasons, but it could be all there is."

He had a point, but even with Tom vouching for Holden there was an instinctive recoil from the thought of going there, whether it was safe or not, a heady mix of queasiness and fascination at the thought of being among a victim's family. JJ said, "I'll buy the book and I'll consider it. But I might just see what I can do for myself first."

"He's a good man, JJ, trust me." Tom could see though that his opinion would count for only so much, that JJ operated further to the edges than he'd ever need to go and that he'd find his own way. And Tom had never killed anyone either, an absence of knowledge that was visible in his face, leaving him with only half the story. Seeing that perhaps and deferring, he said, "But if you do decide not to go, you know you always have my number."

"Thanks." JJ remembered the phone conversation they'd had a short while before and added, "Speaking of which, one more thing. When I called earlier you said no one was trying to kill me *either*. What did you mean by that?"

"Of course, I should have mentioned it sooner." Tom paused, thinking about it like he was only just seeing himself how it tied in with what they'd been discussing. "I told you we'd noticed that some very minor people had been taken down. Well, by the same token, we've been surprised to see some pretty major people acting like there's nothing to worry about."

"Like who?"

"Esther Sanderton, Nick Hooper, Elliot. The rumor mill has everyone diving for cover, but that's not what's happening on the ground, not that we can see anyway."

JJ made to reply, but the girl in the ethnic mix suddenly walked over and spoke to Tom. "Excuse me, do you work here?"

"No, I don't," he said, smiling, looking charmed by the mistake.

She looked put out by his response and like she hadn't quite understood said anyway, "Only I'm looking for a particular book on India, by somebody Fox."

"I know the one you mean. Louisa Fox. It came out quite recently." The girl smiled and followed Tom back to the shelf, where he started searching for the book with her, chattering away, another of his desert-flower friendships springing up over a few minutes.

JJ looked on, bemused again by Tom, too big a personality to be in that line of work. And while he waited he turned over the implications of what he'd just been told. The system wasn't out of control, it was still working fine, but for some unknown reason he'd been cut out of it, along with all those minor players Tom had talked about and a few selected others, Viner among them.

But the mention of Esther's name in particular made him think there might be some other way out. If he could trust anyone it was Esther; she knew the ropes and would at least lay it down for him how it was, let him know how real his options were. If the past was anything to go by she'd probably help him too, use her own connections with Berg as much as she could. Suddenly she was looking like his strongest contact, saving him from the mind tricks of Holden and Bostridge's family.

Tom came back over, having found the book for the girl.

"You missed your vocation," JJ said, smiling.

Tom beamed back. "Can't help myself. I just love these eccentric English girls."

"The people you mentioned . . ."

"All still in London."

"So they know they're okay," he said, the fact sinking in properly for the first time that he was in danger, just as Holden had said, a contract on him as real and immutable as those he carried out himself. It didn't seem to mean anything though, especially now, chinks of daylight appearing. "I'll give it some thought," he added, almost to himself.

Tom smiled but said, "Maybe you should get some sleep first. You look beat."

"Yeah, maybe I'll do that. And thanks, Tom. Drinks are on me next time."

He nodded, a tacit acknowledgment of their strange relationship, said, "Take care, JJ," and turned and breezed out of the shop, back into the September sunlight.

JJ bought the book and, once outside, ripped out the page he needed and dropped the rest into a trash can, folding up the details of the Copley Inn and putting them in his inside jacket pocket. He hailed a cab and asked for his hotel, settling back in the seat, looking at the crowded streets full of beautiful girls brought out by the sunshine.

He needed to sleep, reminded of it only by Tom's com-

ment about looking tired. A night had passed without sleep
since he'd been at Viner's, but he hadn't noticed it until now,
the sensation of life draining away from his muscles, a mental state that was like the beginning of lucid dreaming.

So he needed to sleep, and then according to Tom he
needed to see Holden. And maybe Tom had a point. Holden
was the only one who'd come up with anything for him so
far, and if Tom was right, he was the one who'd be best
placed to help. JJ still balked at the idea though, partly unnerved because of the way Holden had contacted him,
mainly because of Bostridge's family.

He thought back to the hit itself, to the strange girl in
Bostridge's room, to the troubled flight on which he'd met
Aurianne again. And there'd been a picture of his family in
Bostridge's wallet, though JJ couldn't remember now what
they'd looked like, a blank that made it worse.

Because in there among the deeply buried superstition and
the desire not to make connections was an impulse just as
strong, a ghoulish curiosity to see them, to see what their
lives had become because of him. He was just a gun, but beneath the surface the temptation to see what he'd wrought
by being that gun was ever present, a temptation that he felt
in his bones it was wrong to yield to, wrong for everyone but
particularly for them, real people, a woman who'd lost her
husband, kids who'd lost their father.

And despite what Tom had said, there was no need for it
either, because there were people in London, people who
could help him whether they liked it or not, help him in what
mattered: getting to Berg. Most of all, there was Esther, the
beautiful Esther as Danny liked to call her, the only constant
he had left, perhaps the person who could help him most,
give him the right pointers.

But if he wanted Esther's help he knew he'd be better off moving quickly, going there straight away, putting the sleep on hold for just a little while longer. And if it turned out she couldn't help him after all, then he'd still have that page in his pocket, which was where he wanted to keep it given the choice, folded away, unexploited.

He leaned forward and said, "I've changed my mind." He gave Esther's address then, the cabbie shrugging in response and cutting south and west on a series of side streets.

6

He got out of the cab at the far end of the street where Esther lived, two identical rows of white Regency houses, Esther's the second from the far end. He walked casually, taking in the other houses, the cars parked along both sides, checking for any activity.

The only thing standing out was a guy sitting in a car about halfway down, on the opposite side and facing Esther's house. Short of sitting in a van with tinted windows, he couldn't have made it more obvious, but JJ paid him no attention. At a guess he was probably one of Tom's colleagues anyway.

JJ kept it relaxed, smooth, like he was just someone using the street as a shortcut, even giving the appearance of passing Esther's house, waiting until he was on top of it before making a move. It would have taken the watcher in the car a moment or two to realize JJ had stepped up to the columned portico and rung the bell, and by that time he'd have been out of camera shot.

JJ waited there, listening, wondering how she'd react to someone being at her door. He'd have been cautious at the best of times and he'd already reckoned on the possibility of her not answering at all, but with almost no delay the door was suddenly open and she was standing there, like she'd been expecting flowers or a delivery.

It took a second for her to respond, a second in which they stood facing each other, her face registering his presence. She was still beautiful, her dark hair cut short, the light trace of freckles on her skin, full soft lips, but it had been a few years since he'd seen her and he could see now that perhaps she wouldn't wear well, that age wouldn't suit the youthful features.

She looked better when she smiled though, stepping back to let him in. Once he was inside she closed the door and turned to face him. He smiled a little at her expression, keeping eye contact, and then she said quietly, "Thank God," and put her arms around him, pulling herself against him. It was the first real physical contact he'd had since holding the American kid's ropy shoulders the previous afternoon, trying to stop him from vomiting. And it felt good, because he was tired and because she was warm and comfortable against him, an easy intimacy reawakened.

It was a reminder too that their brief relationship had never run its course, that practicalities had gotten in the way but that they'd both seen it as unfinished business, something they'd return to once they'd gotten themselves established. Even now, after too long an interval, there was still something unspoken there, a closeness on hold.

When she finally pulled away she looked at him and said as if to explain herself, "I heard you were one of the people in danger."

"I am," he said. "Or at least, I think I am. I was hoping you might shed some light on it."

She smiled and said, "Come on through," and took him by the arm into the living room.

He could hear water running as they passed the bottom of the stairs, and once they were sitting down he said, "Who else is in the house?"

"Just my boyfriend. Don't worry, he's taking a bath, he'll be forever. Would you like a drink?" She was about to get up again, but he stopped her with a hand gesture, watched her relax back into the sofa.

"I don't want to stay long. It's not good for you to have me here."

"Oh, I don't know." She smiled knowingly. "I'm sure between the two of us we could fend off any attackers." He eased back into the armchair, she lifted her bare feet under her on the sofa, and the two of them stared at each other for a while. It felt good to be sitting here with her, as if the problem was already fading.

She was wearing loose cotton cargo pants but a fitted T-shirt, an enticing relief map of her breasts and stomach, stirring his memory.

"You look great," he said.

Esther returned the pointless compliment. "You've worn pretty well yourself."

He nodded before gesturing upward with his eyes and saying, "What about him? Is it serious?"

"Not settling-down serious, if that's what you mean. And you? Anyone on the go?"

He thought of Aurianne and thought better of mentioning her, but like she'd read his expression Esther's face fell, showing she knew automatically what was hidden in his delayed response. "Oh God," she said as if the realization made her sick. He smiled weakly in response because of how predictable it seemed now and the way he'd hoped against it being true the night before. It was what happened. Esther knew it, he knew it, they all did.

"I found her this morning, raped, interrogated, shot through the head. She didn't even know what I did." He felt torn up again suddenly, the slight distance already making him feel nauseated and bitter for having led her to that.

"Were you close?" Esther asked, avoiding the pat sympathy that anyone else might have offered.

"Not settling-down close," he replied. "But she was a beautiful person. And if she hadn't been involved with me she still would be."

Esther nodded, not saying anything at first, and then, "How about that drink? I've got some Talisker."

"In that case . . . " He smiled, brushing off the air of melancholy, and she got up and left the room, returning a minute later with the bottle and two glasses. "Still like it neat?"

"Of course."

"Good," she said, pouring out two hefty measures. "Richard likes it with ice and water, the heathen."

"The lightweight," JJ added, guessing Richard was the boyfriend in the bath.

"Exactly." She raised her glass. "To us."

"Sounds good to me." He took a swig of the whisky, the heat spreading down his gullet and settling into his stomach, a healing warmth, like its absence had been the only thing wrong with him. He looked at her then, curled up on the sofa again, nursing the tumbler in both hands, relaxed. "So tell me, how come you haven't gone to ground?"

She shrugged in response and said, "I wasn't aware I
needed to. We were told the threat was to Viner and everyone
connected with him. Philip knew he might be a target by association. You have heard about Philip?" JJ nodded, and she
continued as if it didn't really concern her that much. "They
got him two days ago apparently."

"Who?"

"The Russians," she said like it was an unnecessary clarifi-
cation.

"But who? It would have to be someone major."

She shrugged again and said, "It's not really my area of
expertise." She sipped at her whisky and added, "I'm sorry, J,
I'm not being much use, am I?"

"It's not your fault." It had crossed his mind a moment
before that she knew the truth about Berg, the way she was
so casual about him being dead, but the more he thought
about it, if she'd been lying she'd have laid it on thick. She
simply didn't know anything, which left him wondering
what he'd hoped to get from her, other than to escape the
sense of being isolated for a while, to spend some time with
her, someone he had a real history with, someone in whose
company there seemed to be other futures.

"What will you do?"

He shook his head, still lost in thought.

"Stay alive," he offered finally. "I don't know. Kill the people trying to kill me."

"But you don't know who it is."

"Not yet, but it's not the Russians."

"Then who?"

"I don't know." He didn't want to mention Berg, mainly
because he was certain now she didn't know anything. He
wouldn't have mentioned it anyway though, a professional

veneer of suspicion and doubt that was common to everyone in the business, a corrective to set against his own intuition, just as, no matter what she felt about him, a part of her would still be treating him as a potential adversary.

"You should take a holiday," she said, echoing Danny. "A couple of weeks in some resort. It might have blown over by then, and even if it hasn't, at least we'll have a better idea of what's going on." He wondered whether the *we* referred to the two of them or whether more likely it was collective. After all, she was an employee, not freelance, and like all employees had a tendency to slip into the comfort blanket of the organization, forgetting that it was just as likely to smother as to protect.

"No, I know I should take a holiday, but I have some leads and I'd rather follow them while they're still alive." He didn't really have any leads though, apart from the one he wanted to avoid, Holden, the Bostridge connection.

It had been that wish to avoid the trip to Vermont that had brought him to Esther, convincing himself that she'd be able to help in some way. But maybe she couldn't, and if she couldn't there was no one else he could think of, certainly no one he could trust as much as her.

As if reading his thoughts then she said helpfully, "I could make some inquiries, low-key, see if I turn anything up."

"Do you think you'll get anything? I got the impression things had shut down tight."

"For the most part," she said. "There are people I can contact though. Janet Dyson's an old Russian hand; she might be able to tell me something." He nodded though he didn't recognize the name, then felt his thoughts stumble and pile up into each other as he heard Esther ask, "Where are you staying?"

"What?" He'd heard her but had automatically stalled, deciphering what it meant for her to have asked that simple question, where was he staying? She would never have asked it normally, would never have expected an answer either unless she thought she'd caught him unawares, particularly at a time like this.

"In case I find anything out," she said, "where can I reach you?"

He was stunned, stunned that she'd fooled him, that perhaps his thoughts were muddled enough to have been lulled by her familiarity and warmth. He played on the air of confusion, on her supposition that he wasn't thinking clearly, answering absentmindedly, "Of course. I'm at the Halkin, for the next couple of days anyway."

"I love the Halkin," she said, smiling, the familiar Esther again, the possibility there that she'd simply made a mistake, not thought of the implications. It seemed unlikely though. "A great place to eat too."

"Yeah, it's my first time back there in a few years. I'd forgotten how nice it is." He looked at the whisky in his glass and drained it, sitting forward, more businesslike. "Speaking of which, I should go. Like I said, it's not a good idea for you to have me here." He stood and added, "Try your Russian contact though."

"I'll do it right now." She leaned forward and picked up the phone.

"I'll see myself out then." She raised her hand, taking his in it and holding it against her lips for a second, what looked like real affection again. And maybe it was real affection, heightened because she knew she was about to betray him. He knew how it was, nothing personal, never anything personal when it came to business. For whatever reason, because she was involved with the true process or because she'd been fed some alternative truth, she was willing to conspire now to have him killed, an enemy to be eradicated.

"Be careful," she said as she let his hand go, another genuine sentiment from the past, like all the others she'd used to conceal the reality that was there between them. And he'd fallen for it, till she'd slipped and made that one mistake, asking him where he was staying, leaving him disappointed, and insulted that she'd thought him capable of missing it.

He smiled at her and walked out as she began to punch the numbers on the phone. Opening the front door and closing it again without leaving, he stepped into the small recess for coats to one side of it. Esther was already speaking a little too cheerily to the imaginary Janet in the background. He listened as he stood among the coats, one of them full of the stale stench of cigarettes, another giving off a trace of some fragrance, a man's aftershave perhaps.

Esther's voice grew louder as she stepped out of the living room to check that he'd gone and then, once she was satisfied, stopped altogether. He eased his hand inside his jacket and pulled his gun. When he heard her speak again she was back in the living room, talking quietly. He stepped into the open, a couple of paces on his toes across the black-and-white mosaic floor, stopping near the bottom of the stairs once she was in earshot.

"I don't know," she was saying. "If it wasn't Danny, maybe he has someone who's better informed." A pause and then, "It doesn't matter anyway. He's staying at the Halkin." The obvious question from the person at the other end. "Yes, I'm certain. Of course, it's possible he was bluffing but I can't see it; I know him too well. And anyway, why would he suspect me?" There was the insult put into words, leaving

him not so much hurt as baffled that she could have come to
think so little of him, that he could have thought he'd known
her so well.

He listened in again but was distracted by some movement
on the landing at the top of the stairs, the boyfriend she'd
said would take forever in the bath. He was probably moving
from the bathroom to the bedroom, but JJ began to ease
backward just in case.

He was almost back to the door when the guy appeared at
the top of the stairs, wearing a short white dressing gown,
towel-drying long black hair, bits of it straggling across his
face. He was unshaven, swarthy, for some reason suggesting
someone who worked in some branch of the media, advertis-
ing or music or something like that.

JJ responded to the sight of him by stopping his retreat
and standing casually with the gun out of view at his side,
like he was meant to be there, biding his time. And as the
guy saw him JJ smiled and nodded, the passing nod men give
to each other, and gestured silently with his free hand to
show that Esther was on the phone. The guy acknowledged
silently that he understood but he stayed where he was for a
second, JJ mentally urging him to continue on his way to the
bedroom.

He started down the stairs though, saying in a hushed
voice when he was halfway down, "I don't think we've met.
I'm Richard." It was a voice that didn't fit with the way he
looked, a cleric's voice.

In the other room he heard Esther say urgently, "I'll call
you back." JJ shot the guy in the middle of the chest, knocking him backward, sliding down the stairs on his back then,
like he'd missed a step and lost his footing. JJ moved quickly
to the living room, firing a couple of shots blind as he

walked in, a third as he got her in his sights, straight into the
back of her head, sending her crashing to the floor and
against one of the armchairs, where she lay immediately mo-
tionless, contorted like her neck was broken, her blood like
oil stains on the blue fabric of the chair cover.

The guy was still gurgling on the stairs behind him, but JJ
left him and walked in to take a closer look at Esther. Her
face was bloodied, and one of his blind shots had caught her
in the shoulder, a piece of luck that had probably given him
the edge. Her gun was in her hand, pretty impressive considering how quickly she'd had to move, pretty impressive, pe-
riod.

They'd had a conversation once in a pub not far from
here, about who'd win out if they both had contracts on each
other. He couldn't remember what conclusion they'd come
to, if any, but it had seemed hypothetical enough back then
to keep them entertained over a couple of drinks.

Wider opinion had it different, but he'd always thought
her the better all-around operator, even up to the way she'd
caught him out there, but by the only absolute measure she
was the one who was dead. If she hadn't asked about the hotel, hadn't raised his suspicions, she could have put a bullet
in his back as he'd walked up the hallway, an error of judgment inexcusable for someone of her caliber, no matter what
the basis.

He picked up the phone and pressed to redial the last
number. As soon as it rang a woman answered, efficient
sounding but giving just a simple "Hello?" It wasn't a voice
he recognized.

"This is Hoffman. I have a message for Philip Berg."
There was silence for a while at the other end, like she was
consulting with someone or weighing how to respond. Fi-

nally she said, "Go on," no discernible tone in her voice.

"Okay. There's no charge for the one who raped my girl-friend, but he owes me the regular fee for Wilson and Sander-ton. Tell him I'll collect in person." He hung up then and threw the phone on the sofa, looking once more at Esther, feeling coldly triumphant, surprising considering it was someone he'd thought he cared about, surprising too that he felt nothing else. He checked the boyfriend on the stairs as he passed, dead now, his dressing gown up around his shoulders where he'd slid down away from it; he was a hairy guy.

And then he left, stunned that he could have been so wrong, that she could so easily have turned against him, questioning whether he could ever have turned like that him-self, against someone he'd known that well. He doubted it, but then he wasn't an organization player, the same factor that had helped him stay alive, the factor that allowed him his own thoughts, that meant he didn't always take the rec-ommended path, the plus side of his isolated existence.

He crossed the street right outside the house and stood on the other side for a moment, making like he wasn't sure which way to go, giving the impression that he was preoccu-pied. And he maintained that expression as he walked up the street, waiting until he was right alongside the car, betting that the guy inside would be averting his eyes too as JJ passed.

It was the second dummy he'd thrown the guy in no time at all, but it still worked well enough. Within seconds JJ was sitting in the passenger seat with the gun pressed into the guy's ribs, the barrel tugging at the white cotton of his shirt, the guy shocked and reacting like most people did to the bruising up-close presence of a gun, holding his breath, like he wanted nothing to move, like stillness was his only hope.

He was young, probably even younger than Tom, which explained why he was on a detail like that, sitting in some quiet London street taking pictures of people coming and going at a particular house.

"Okay," said JJ, once he was happy the situation was stable. "I have a question for you. Which state does Tom Furst come from?" The guy turned his head slightly, still tense, like he had an injured neck. He looked puzzled. "Just answer the question."

He still looked uneasy, like it was a trick question, answering slowly, "I believe, sir, that Tom Furst comes from New Hampshire." His own accent was southern, the Carolinas or somewhere like that.

"How do you know that?"

"Because he's my colleague," he said, and like he suddenly understood what JJ was doing added, "At the embassy."

"Good. As long as you don't try anything stupid, those answers just saved your life." With his free hand JJ leaned over and picked up the camera, checking the number of shots taken. He put the camera back in his lap then and said, "Very carefully, and I mean very carefully, wind off the film and hand it to me." The guy did as he said, his hands steady, no sign of the way he had to be feeling.

JJ slipped the film into his pocket.

"Now give me the roll you completed before this, just that roll; you can keep the others." The American moved his hand slowly to the door compartment and lifted out a small black film container, holding it between his thumb and finger like it was something dangerous that had to be handled with care. JJ took it and asked, "Where's your gun?" The guy gestured toward the glove compartment. JJ opened it and took out the gun, still in its shoulder holster. "Mobile?"

The guy reached again into the door compartment, handing the phone over with the same precision movements. "And keys?" The guy allowed himself a little smile this time as he handed over the keys, perhaps again because he understood what JJ was doing or because he realized no one was ever that cautious with an imminent corpse.

The operation complete, JJ relaxed a little, even easing the pressure of the silencer against the guy's body. "What's your name?"

"Randal, sir," he answered automatically, adding a little hesitantly, "Lucas Randal."

JJ nodded.

"Well, Lucas, my name's William Hoffman. People call me JJ. And at the moment people are trying to kill me, but if I survive, as I intend to, then consider me as owing you a favor." Randal looked at him, that puzzled expression back on his face. JJ smiled and said, "I appreciate this leaves you with some explaining to do, so maybe one day I'll make it up to you. Ask Tom: he'll explain how useful my favors can be."

"Thank you, sir, I'll do that."

JJ smiled again, amused and impressed by Randal's southern manners, thanking the man who'd just robbed him at gunpoint. He opened the door, easing himself carefully from the car, keeping the gun on Randal, holding the three items against his stomach with the other hand.

"I'll leave these on the street corner. Don't get out of the car until I'm out of sight." Randal nodded in response. "Oh, when you call in, you might earn some brownie points if you tell them the two people in the house are dead."

"Should I mention your name?"

"Doesn't matter to me. Probably better for you if you don't. Except to Tom of course." He closed the door and walked away, leaving the gun, mobile phone, and keys on the street corner, walking further before hailing a cab on a busier street.

With the afternoon passing but still warm, he left the films to develop at an express photo shop and crossed the street to a coffee bar, sitting in the window with a cup of lemon and ginger, watching the mix of tourists and business-people moving along at conflicting speeds.

He'd been tempted to go back to the hotel for an hour but had decided against the sleeping draft of a comfortable room, silence, a bed. He still felt okay, but he knew the need for sleep had to be building up inside him, ready to catch him off guard if he gave it a chance, and he couldn't afford to do that, couldn't afford to let the momentum go.

As it was, they were as much in the dark about him as he was about them. Perhaps his speed and the steady attrition would begin to get to them, draw Berg into mistakes, even out in the open.

And even if it wasn't Berg's game, he felt that if he could get to Berg he'd at least have some chance of freeing himself up. If it was the whole organization out to get him it would be harder, but except in the minds of the paranoid it was never the whole organization, only factions, and factions could be dealt with.

So for now at least, on a strangely aggressive high after killing Esther, he felt almost like he had the upper hand, that if he kept going there wouldn't be much they could do to take him down. He felt more the hunter than the hunted, fighting in his own anonymous environment, as far away as it was possible to be from the place where Holden wanted him, and no need for his help either.

He was back at the photo shop early, hyped on the low-level exhilaration that was creeping through him, eager to see what information the films yielded. He waited surrounded by a group of Japanese girls who spoke to each other in quiet tones, talking like they were trying to make sense of all the minor mysteries they were encountering there.

They got their photographs first and looked through them straight away, enthusiastic, talking in rapid bursts punctuated by gasps of enlightenment, like the key to understanding the city was hidden in those pictures.

When JJ got his photographs, he too looked through them in the shop and was struck after half a dozen or so by how mystified the Japanese tourists would have been by the sight of them, all of the same nondescript house, the people caught in them equally hard to differentiate.

There were quite a few people in suits, himself included, a smaller number in casual clothes, the long-haired boyfriend going out for the paper, none of Esther herself. Most of the suits he recognized as other people who worked for Berg, people like Hooper, Elliot, Parker-Hall, a skinny Kiwi guy whose name he couldn't remember.

In among them though was a bigger fish, Stuart Pearson, someone who was at least on a level with Berg and maybe farther up the food chain still. It was unmistakably him, the cropped sandy hair, bald on top, the small silver-rimmed glasses, the look about him of a doctor or lawyer, of someone working within some tightly defined professional structure.

JJ had never spoken to him, but he'd seen him a couple of times, knew where he lived too. And he knew that out of all the people in the pictures, Pearson would be the one with answers, about how far it all went, whether he could stop it by getting to Berg, maybe even where Berg was hiding out.

He didn't know enough about the guy to know whether it would be easy to get that information, but he was in the mood now to get it whatever it took, angered, feeling full of poison. And he seemed to remember Pearson had kids too; so as long as he got him at home it was just a matter of finding his threshold, JJ free to operate without restraint, answerable to no one but himself, to a conscience which had long been reduced to the role of passive observer.

7

Pearson lived in a redbrick Victorian terrace that in any other city would have been home to students but in London was undoubtedly worth a fortune. JJ was thinking about it as he stepped from the cab, how people could live in places which had nothing attractive about them except the financial value of the property itself.

People worked hard, long hours, fighting their way across the city and back each day, worrying about crime and their kids, paying vast amounts to live in houses which would have been shunned by their own class at the time they'd been built. His place in Geneva wasn't perfect but he was in no doubt as to who had the better deal.

It was only as the cab eased away and he started up the steps to the door that it occurred to him Pearson might still be at work. Even worse, if he had kids maybe his wife had given up work and JJ would have to spend time with her before Pearson got back.

He rang the bell and listened. He could hear children in-

side, and a woman who sounded foreign, a nanny probably.
Then much louder and closer he heard another voice, Pearson's he assumed, calling to the nanny that he'd get the door.

JJ drew his gun quickly and as the door opened stepped
immediately into the gap, denying Pearson the obvious de-
fense of slamming it again. So by the time Pearson's
thoughts had caught up JJ was already in the hallway with
the gun easily visible.

"You people," JJ said then, shocked by the way both Esther and Pearson had flung their doors open unchecked,
"doesn't security mean anything to you?"

Caught off guard Pearson reacted with a look of scorn
and said, "What are you doing here?" The tone was wrong,
like JJ was some social outcast gate-crashing a party, making
him wonder whether, despite his visit to Esther, Pearson fully
appreciated what was going on. More likely though, he simply hadn't seen the gun, so JJ closed the door behind him
and pointed it casually at Pearson's stomach.

It seemed to answer the question, and for a few seconds
the two of them stood saying nothing, Pearson still dressed
as he had been in Randal's photographs, minus the pale gray
suit jacket now and the tie, the collar of his blue shirt open.

From the corner of his eye JJ could see the nanny fussing
around children at the distant kitchen table. It was only a
glance but Pearson caught it and said quickly, his tone suddenly conciliatory, "My study's upstairs. Perhaps we can talk
in there."

"Lead the way," JJ replied, confident he wouldn't have
any problems, and followed him up the stairs, keeping a
couple of paces behind, letting the gun fall to his side rather
than walk like a movie villain with it pointing at Pearson's
back.

The house was better inside, modern, simple, like it had

been decorated by someone with an eye for design. Even the study avoided the traditional walnut and leather JJ had expected from the look of Pearson himself. Instead it was all light, brightly colored furnishings, a beech desk, a wooden seagull hanging from the ceiling.

JJ pointed at a small yellow sofa and waited till Pearson was sitting before perching on the edge of the desk. He was still looking around, noticing the children's books among the others on the shelves, a teddy bear half out of sight behind the yellow sofa. Finally he made eye contact and said, "Why does Berg want me dead?"

"What are you talking about? *Berg's* dead."

"That line's getting tiresome. Now let's save time: I know Berg's alive and I know he wants me dead. What I don't know is why."

Pearson responded, his tone clipped and harsh, "Okay, Hoffman, I won't insult your intelligence, but kindly do me the honor of not insulting mine." He sounded like a lawyer now as well as looking like one, a sense of gravitas about him that was as incongruous in the child-friendly surroundings as JJ with his gun. "If you place the needs of Russian Mafia factions above those of the British Government you can hardly be surprised at the outcome."

"I don't put anyone's needs above anyone else's," JJ said, not making the more obvious objection that he had no Mafia connections.

Undeterred and combative, Pearson countered dismissively, "Of course! Your famous contractual status. But I'm afraid being a dual-nationality mercenary offers you no dispensation. You take the Queen's shilling, you abide by the Queen's rules. Viner knew that, you knew it, everyone connected knew it."

JJ didn't respond at first, confused by how certain Pearson was, and by his disdain and bloody-mindedness in the face of a gun. Then he realized that Pearson really didn't have any idea what was going on, that he'd been fed a story and had taken it whole, choking on it, losing any sense of reason he might have had.

"You're wrong," JJ said eventually. "Yeah, I kill people for money, but that's all I do. I don't deal information or play politics, I just kill the people I'm paid to kill. And Viner and the other people who worked with him . . . Why would any of them have played games? What could they have gained from it that they didn't have already?"

Pearson's expression changed to one of mild condescension and he said, "Taking what you say at face value, I am willing to accept the possibility of your being an unwitting pawn in Viner's treachery, and if that really is the case then I do sympathize with your plight. But the die is cast. It's in Berg's hands now."

"That's why I intend to get to him."

"A fanciful thought," Pearson said, smiling, the condescension oozing like liquid around his words. "But Berg's protection isn't even in our hands. An overreaction in my view but, without knowing the full extent of Viner's network, Philip thought it safer to be at a step's remove."

"What are you talking about?"

"I'm sorry, I do sympathize, as I've made clear, but I really don't think I'm in a position to help you any further."

JJ had to admire his gall or self-belief or whatever it was making him talk like that when he was the one in the position of weakness. "You seem to misunderstand something, Pearson. I didn't come here for help, I came here to get information. And I'll get it, because out there maybe it's my life in danger but in here it's yours. And, if necessary, it's your children's too."

Pearson snapped back, "Leave my children out of this." A knee-jerk response, a reaction so immediate and powerful that for a moment he looked ready to launch himself from the sofa.

JJ responded just as forcefully though, suddenly sick of Pearson's attitude, the words spitting out rapid-fire. "No! No one gets left out, not Viner, not my girlfriend, not me! Berg wants me dead. Well I have news—I've killed four people today and I'm nowhere near finished. I'll kill you and your kids and the nanny and your neighbors if I feel like it, and I'll keep killing people till they get the message that they picked on the wrong guy!" It worked, Pearson looking truly rattled for the first time. JJ added more calmly, "Now, how much do you love your children?"

"I love my children a great deal," Pearson said, earnest, the first indication of a real person beneath all that bluster. "But I can't give you information I don't have."

"I'll be the judge of that. What were you discussing with Esther today?"

Pearson was suddenly too busy being compliant to notice the implication of JJ's question, that he was getting intelligence from somewhere. "I was keeping them up to speed; there'll be some restructuring once this is out of the way."

"Who's protecting Berg?"

"I don't know. I don't even know if it's a case of him being protected." He was lying even now, a built-in inclination that was only slowly yielding.

"So take a guess. If he's being protected, who might be protecting him?"

"I don't know," Pearson said again, more insistent, an air of convincing desperation creeping into his voice.

It was amazing to see, this Achilles' heel opening up steadily before him, concern for his family gradually bringing Pearson around. Some of the people JJ killed professionally had families of course, but it was rare for him to kill family men in their own homes. He met most of them in anonymous places, in hotels, in transit, away from the kinds of witnesses who might act irrationally.

Pearson wasn't a hit though, he was an information source, and the keys to that information were being fed in the kitchen directly below them. JJ didn't want it to come to that, didn't believe either that it would even come close, but he would if he had to and Pearson knew that too, now at least.

JJ plucked a small picture frame off the desk and looked at it, a smiling boy and girl of school age, a baby sitting vacantly between them. "Nice kids," he said before putting it back down. Pearson didn't respond, he merely stared at him, calculating perhaps or bewildered, all his arrogance faded. "I killed a kid once a few years back. I say a kid—he was only, say, eight or nine, but he was off his head and waving an AK-47. So I don't know if that counts but he looked like a kid when he was dead, harmless, innocent. Then I suppose most dead people look harmless; it's the nature of the condition."

"Please . . ."

The interjection was desperate, emotionally punch-drunk, but JJ continued, "I've never killed a real kid, you know, an untainted kid, and I have no doubt that it would haunt me. But, you see, that's the trouble with me. I'd rather be haunted and alive than without blemish and dead. So you really need to start thinking, or we're going down to the kitchen and I'll line them up and kill them one by one till it comes back to you." Pearson was slowly shaking his head, eyes downcast. JJ coaxed him further. "Think hard. Where might Berg be, and if he's being protected by someone who might that be?"

He was convinced there was something in the last question, the fact that Pearson had described Berg's protection as not being in their hands. If Berg had simply gone to ground Pearson would have said as much, so Berg was definitely being sheltered by some third party.

"I don't know anything for sure," Pearson said eventually. "It's not my area and you must know how Berg is for keeping a lid on things."

"But?" said JJ, speeding him along.

"In the last few months Philip has been nurturing some high-level links in Russia. I believe it's how the situation being dealt with presently first came to light."

"FSB links?" Pearson shook his head, like it still hurt him even to be giving this much. "Mafia links?" JJ asked, incredulous at the brazenness of it.

"It's a blanket term, but yes."

"So Viner gets airbrushed for supposed Mafia links while Berg relies on the same links for protection and no one thinks to question his operation?"

"That's a simplification, and you know it is." Any hint of common sense was always dismissed as simplification. "And I don't know for certain that he's being protected by them at the moment. You asked me to guess."

"Who is it?"

"I don't know. I really don't know," he said, emphasizing the words. "And I can't guess. For God's sake, your guess is probably a damn sight better than mine when it comes to the Russians."

"Ah, but I have a tendency to simplify things."

Pearson looked at him like he wasn't quite sure where JJ was coming from. He seemed to be struck by some thought or other then and said, "You don't stand a chance. You know that, don't you? You can keep killing everyone you encounter but it won't get you to Berg, and as long as he's alive you're dead."

He had a point, particularly now, with unknown Russians entering his equation on Berg's side. But that was no reason not to keep going.

JJ shot him in the chest, the force momentarily stapling him to the sofa, his shirt bloodied and wet. He spared him the head shot, thinking of his wife or whoever discovered him, so for a while Pearson sat there staring at him with a look of total shock, like he'd believed the information would buy his own life as well as his children's. Or perhaps he'd thought it possible to reason and discuss his way out of it, that JJ could be drawn into reasoning and discussing too, and death made to creep away again.

But whatever the cause of that dumbfounded expression, it probably served as some explanation for the way he'd been with JJ from the beginning. Pearson had no idea what it was really like; he'd never been any closer to risk than sticking pins in maps. And then he'd come up against it in his own home and realized too late that he was out of his depth, like a peacetime general thrown into a guerrilla campaign. No wonder he looked shell-shocked.

After a few seconds though, he began to come out of it, his eyes working rapid expressions as everything else shut down around them, his mind finding a focus one more time. He began to mouth something and JJ moved toward him. Normally when people had the chance to speak it was something about it not being fair, like dying was a game where the best team always won. Pearson though said in a breathy whisper, "Don't hurt my children."

"I won't," JJ answered him, though in one way or another it seemed a little late for assurances.

He'd considered not killing Pearson but, as compliant as he'd seemed at the end, the fact was JJ had forced his way into his home, held him at gunpoint, threatened his kids. Part of the art of staying alive was knowing that a man like Pearson would never have let that go. He'd have waited for the right opportunity maybe, but he'd have taken his revenge sooner or later.

JJ watched him die, checked his pulse to be certain, then stood and looked around the room, a fresh early-morning quality about it. He pulled the cord hanging from the wooden seagull and watched its wings and body move in an easy rhythmic flight that took it nowhere. He locked the door as he left and took the key with him, mindful that it was a room the kids were probably in and out of all the time.

He moved quickly down the stairs then and out of the house, the same noises still constant in the kitchen behind him. And outside he moved briskly along the street, the sky edging toward darkness, a hollow chill in the air that gave the lie to the summery warmth of the afternoon.

He'd walked twenty yards or so when he noticed a woman coming toward him in a smart business suit, glasses, attractive but severely professional looking. He knew instinctively that it was Pearson's wife, and as she got closer thought he could even see a resemblance between her and the girl in the photograph.

He studied her face in the moments as they passed. She looked full of fatigue, heavy with it, like she couldn't wait to get in and relax, take her shoes off, have a drink, mess around with the kids, simple pleasures that were a long way off now.

A little farther along the street he turned and watched as

she walked up the steps, opened the door. It felt like if he waited there a few minutes more he'd hear a scream break through the stillness of the September air. It didn't happen like that in real life though; in real life there was only the depressing silent yelling of the street itself, bleak, desolate.

He kept walking, dragged down inside by the thought of that woman, and by the memory of her husband's final words to him before being shot. It had all been a waste, a pointless cavalry charge that had gotten him no nearer. And all because he'd wanted to avoid the awkwardness of meeting a victim's family, the irony of it claustrophobic, and even more so now because he would have to meet them anyway.

Perhaps Pearson had been right to be contemptuous of him for being nothing more than a killer, someone who'd forgotten how to think beyond killing. Holden was the only option, something he'd already acknowledged to himself, and yet he'd refused to act on it, a day's delay at a cost of three people, one of whom had been a friend, another as unconnected as Aurianne had been.

Pearson JJ normally wouldn't have regretted; he was the kind of sneering, inflated guy who invited violence. But he'd killed him in his home, which made it harder somehow, the knowledge of that brightly colored study that would never be the same, the businesswoman whose life was going into a tailspin even as he walked away from her.

But then people were bereaved all the time; it happened, part of the fabric. And people's lives continued, improved sometimes in unspoken ways, became richer. It was unfortunate but it happened, JJ just one more random cause, in there among cancers and car crashes and countless others. And at least too the children had been spared; she didn't know it but she had that to be thankful for.

A cab pulled up, a guy in a suit stepping out, carrying a briefcase. JJ took the cab on back to his hotel, a long comfortable journey, the streets gradually darkening, lights appearing, the city washing over him as it made its way home. He was tired, left melancholy by the day's events. He needed sleep, to lose himself. And he needed to stop thinking, because every now and then he fell into a cycle of it, turning it all over, attempting to draw it all together, like there were answers inside certain moments, answers to where he'd been and where he was going, answers to who he was.

Probably no one had those answers anyway, no matter what they did for a living, and for the time being at least the only answers that mattered were the ones Holden was offering; the rest was a luxury.

8

He stared at the white clapboard walls beneath the clear blue sky, the russet tones of the surrounding trees, the leaf-strewn lawn. It looked like a house where people were happy, like a house from a hundred American stories where dramas served only as a relief against the return to contentment.

And then in that white clapboard house a phone was ringing and after just a couple of rings a woman answered.

"Good afternoon, this is the Copley Inn. How can I help?" It was what people in big hotels said but this sounded authentic, like the original greeting the business world had based its corporate drill upon.

"I'd like to book a room please, for tomorrow if that's possible."

"My goodness you're lucky," said the woman he already took to be Susan Bostridge though she could have been anybody. "We're full but somebody unexpectedly has to leave tomorrow. Could I take your name please?"

"Yes. William Hoffman," he said, hoping that the person leaving unexpectedly wasn't Holden. Then he realized he'd given his real name, a sudden act of carelessness, perhaps because he was tired. It was a slip that nagged at him as he gave her the rest of his details, finished the niceties, the woman looking forward to seeing him the next evening.

When he put the phone down he folded up the page from the book of New England inns and threw it aside, sliding down the bed, lying there with tiredness bearing down on him like ballast. He drifted in and out of sleep but never for long and never satisfying and by eight he was awake again, a sudden jolt bursting through him like an electric shock, a sense of hollowness, of the blood draining out of his heart and leaving him lifeless.

He reached over and turned off the bedside lamp and lay for a while in the darkness, gauging whether more sleep would come, but his mind was unreeling, chattering away to itself, throwing up the day's events and jarring echoes of the conversations he'd had, snippets of dead people talking.

He got up from the bed and went over to the window, looking at the nightscape of city light and darkness, a darkness that was concealing people's lives, a city he felt isolated from, excluded from even. Years before he'd have been only a phone call away from some of those people, regular people. Somewhere along the line though he'd let them all go, replacing them with people who spoke the same coded language, and now that code was no good.

Maybe some of the old friends were still out there, going through the drill of everyday life. And maybe occasionally they thought fleetingly of him too, on the tube, staring from the office window, the mystery of his whereabouts briefly flickering across their conscious concerns.

It would be good, he thought, on a day like that, between life, to be with some of those friends, to tell them that he was still there, perhaps even in some ways the same person they'd known. It would be good as well to know that in the days following, those people would tell other people and that in some disembodied form his life, the person he'd been ten years before, would be spirited back into existence.

Yet as he thought about it in those terms, he wasn't even certain how he'd changed, or if he'd changed. It was like he'd lost sight of himself, seeing only a shadow moving from place to place, going through the motions, doing just enough to merge with the crowd. Perhaps that was the real change: that he was no longer visible enough to be judged.

He walked back across the room, put the light on, and took a whisky from the minibar. He poured it and knocked it straight back, holding its anesthetic quality in his mouth for a while before letting it trickle down his throat.

He thought idly about how he might contact one of the old friends he'd been thinking of, and about the tattered address book that lay somewhere hidden away at home, beneath photographs and letters and other stored history. It couldn't be that difficult though to track one of them down, even after seven or eight years.

Thinking of different people, faces, vaguer memories, he was suddenly desperate for the contact, mentally scrabbling around before thinking of Jools and how maybe he could find her even without an address book. He almost remembered her parents' address, enough to get the number from directory assistance, and beyond that was easy.

It was ridiculous, he knew that, to get in touch out of the blue after all this time and with only a few hours of one evening left in London. And maybe she wouldn't even want to meet him, her own life moved on as much as his had, a sense of awkwardness that someone like him should want to dig up the past. At the least though he could speak to her, find out.

He got the first number without a problem and dialed, the phone ringing a few times at the other end before her mother answered. The voice sounded familiar but, still unsure that it was her, JJ said, "Hello, is that Mrs. Garland?"

"Yes," the reply came back cautiously as if suspecting an imminent sales pitch.

"Hi. I'm an old college friend of Julia's. I was wondering if you had her number. I have one but it's very old, when she was in North London."

The woman loosened up, like it was the kind of inquiry she was used to dealing with.

"Yes of course. She is still in North London but probably a different number. Let me see . . ." There was a pause and then she reeled it off before saying, "I didn't catch your name?"

"Yes, I'm sorry. It's JJ. We did meet once."

"Yes, I remember. How lovely!" Her tone had shifted again, to one he remembered from his time as a student, as though they were all still precocious children, nothing more. "And what are you doing with yourself now?" Again he liked the sound of the question, the implicit suggestion that he was still too young to have settled into anything like a real career.

"I work for a venture capital company in Zurich."

"How interesting," she said, more likely referring to the location than to the catchall job description. "Well it's lovely to hear from you, JJ. And Julia will be pleased."

He wound up the conversation and dialed again immediately, encouraged. Her phone rang for a long time, long enough for him to be thrown when she answered, initially mistaking her for an answering machine.

"Hello, Julia Garland."

"Hello, Jools. It's JJ."

Her dumbfounded reply came back one word at a time: "Oh. My. God."

He laughed and said, "I know, it's been a while."

"I don't believe it," she said, and then, "Are you in London?"

"Yeah. Yes I am. That's why I'm calling. I know it's getting on but I thought, if you have nothing planned, I'd come over for an hour."

"Of course!" Her response was immediate, insistent, her voice sounding briefly like her mother's. "Do you want me to come and pick you up?"

"No, don't be stupid. I'll get a taxi. I should be there in twenty minutes."

"Great," she said, still sounding shocked. "I'll see you then."

"Maybe if you give me the address?" She laughed and gave it to him, and though he'd said twenty minutes he took a quick shower and changed before going down and jumping in a taxi.

It was completely dark now, the lit city coming into its own. He felt better than he had earlier, because in going to see Jools he could forget for a while what was going on around him, forget that somewhere out there people were actively trying to find and kill him.

Sitting in the dark in the back of his cab, he didn't have to think about strategy and what his plans were. He didn't have to think at all for the next few hours, not about Berg or

Holden or the Bostridges or any of the other people whose names would mean nothing to Jools. He didn't have to think, just reminisce and relax back into easy parts of his past.

The house and the street when he got there were similar to Pearson's, the same overpriced redbrick uniformity, the bleakness tempered though by the darkroom glow of the streetlights. Her house itself looked dark, but when he rang the bell a porch light came on and a hallway light beyond the door.

There was a peephole, and he sensed her checking through it before the door opened. And then she was standing there, unchanged apparently except for the neat bump showing beneath her lambswool pullover.

"You're pregnant," he said, the first words from his mouth.

She smiled and said, "You should've considered becoming a doctor." He smiled too, acknowledging the statement of the obvious. "Come in," she added, stepping aside and closing the door behind him.

There was a moment then when neither of them quite knew what to do. They'd been good friends but now that seemed like a long time ago, and as if they'd forgotten the language of familiarity there was an awkwardness, a shyness even. Finally JJ broached it, laughing and saying, "What are we meant to do here? Kiss? Hug?"

"How about a bit of both?" she said, kissing him on the cheek and holding herself against him for a few seconds, stirring the thought of Esther's Judas greeting earlier that day. When she pulled away she smiled at him and said, "Boy, do you have some explaining to do!"

"Tell me about it."

"Come on then, let's have tea." She led him through to the

kitchen, showing him the other downstairs rooms on the way, one of them still undecorated. It looked like her place somehow, no indication that someone else lived there, raising the question of the expected baby's father, the suggestion that perhaps JJ wasn't the only one with a recent history worth telling.

He sat at the heavy wooden table in the kitchen, a rustic look to the room like part of her wanted to go back and live in Somerset. As she made the tea he said, "So when's the baby due?"

"Second of December." She turned and patted the bump. "So it looks like I'm in for a family Christmas."

"It's amazing," he said, staring at her stomach. "It's just hard to believe you're pregnant, you know, grown up, having a child."

"I don't know about grown up. But I am twenty-nine, not exactly a schoolgirl mother." She poured the water into the teapot and brought it over to the table, then the mugs and milk. Sitting down she said, "Do you want to touch it?"

"Do you mind?"

"Why should I mind?" She smiled and lifted the sweater and T-shirt under it to reveal her rounded, marble-smooth stomach.

"I should warm my hands," he said, rubbing them together. He pulled his chair out and reached over, putting his palm flat on the skin and moving it slowly across the curved world of her body like it was a piece of living sculpture.

There was no kick, no movement, but an overpowering sense all the same of another life enclosed there, another heart beating, another mind already subconsciously recording its mother's moods, environment, sounds, perhaps even the touch of his hand. Unexpectedly he felt himself moved, ambushed by the emotional power of it, his eyes welling up a little without him knowing why.

He looked at her, bemused by his own response to something so commonplace, an unborn child that wasn't even his own, in which he had no investment.

"Well?" Jools could see he was moved, and she looked touched in turn by his response.

"It's beautiful," he said. "I don't know why but it's really beautiful."

She smiled, pleased, and said, "A man who's not afraid of his emotions—now there's a rare thing."

He smiled back. It was a compliment that made him uneasy though. Maybe he wasn't afraid of his emotions, but it was a lack of fear that also manifested itself in ways she would have found completely alien.

Shifting away from himself he said, "What about the father?"

"Shall I pour?" she answered with a wry smile, confirming what he'd thought earlier. She poured the tea but continued dismissively, "To be fair, it was a fling, nothing more, fun for a couple of months but not someone I would have wanted to stay with. It had already fizzled by the time I found out I was pregnant."

"Did you tell him?"

"Oh I told him and he was fine about it, offered to support me and everything, which I declined. Rather thankfully, he seems quite happy to have nothing further to do with it."

He wondered if she was putting a brave face on it, but she seemed at ease with things, too relaxed to be covering her true feelings. He could understand it too from the way she looked because there was a completeness about her, like they hadn't known the whole person back at college but there she was now, all her promise delivered. It made him warm to her even more than he had in his memory.

"Will you be okay financially?"

"Yes I think so," she said, nodding. "I may not look high-powered but I am, and the City's been good to me. Frankly, I could retire now and not worry about holidays or school fees or anything else. As it is I'll work part-time or freelance, employ a good nanny. It's incredible really; my parents are still baffled as to exactly what it is I do and yet I get paid huge amounts of money for it."

"I know what you mean."

Her face was transformed suddenly by another thought. "God, how are your parents? And your little sister!"

"Oh they're all fine," he said, finding it strange to be with someone again who'd met his family, who had access to the lumber room where he kept all those other parts of himself. "My sister's not so little anymore. She's a journalist for Reuters in Hong Kong. My parents are still the same though."

She laughed, overcome with memory, and said, "Remember the summer we came over to your parents' place? What did we call it? The Schloss Dunstoned!"

"The Schloss Dunstoned," he repeated, transported back briefly. "God that seems like forever ago."

She sat smiling, thinking of it, then said, "So what's your excuse? Why did you disappear?"

"I didn't disappear. I just, you know how it is . . . you're so busy doing whatever it is you do." He picked up his tea and took a sip, invigoratingly hot, a blend that had plenty of Darjeeling in it.

He was about to try another feint by commenting on it,

but she got there first, asking, "And what exactly is it that you do?"

"It sounds more exciting than it is," he said, putting the tea down again. "A small venture capital company in Zurich, THS; I'm the H."

"THS," she repeated, clearly not believing him, making him wonder if rumors had ever passed along the grapevine about him. "Funny, I've never heard of it."

"Maybe you haven't been listening hard enough. I did say it was small." He imagined her going into work the next day, making some checks, finding that it existed after all and that he was the H just as he'd said. She was an old friend though, onto something and running with it, uninhibited by any reputation he'd earned since, seeing no need to tread carefully around him like some people would.

"I heard you were a spy or something, or . . ." She trailed off.

He raised his eyebrows, slightly mocking, and pressed her, "Or what?"

"I heard you were a hitman," she said, trying to laugh off the embarrassment of how fanciful it sounded. It sounded fanciful to him too, even after all this time, certain that it was a coincidence, that someone had made it up rather than having heard a proper rumor.

"A hitman?" he said in response, astonished, reinforcing her doubts. "Why would a history graduate become a hitman? How?" Once again it was a good point, one he'd put to himself countless times, never really coming up with an answer. After all, why did anyone end up doing it?

She smiled, deferring and saying, "I know, it's ridiculous. But you can hardly blame people for speculating when no one hears anything for all this time."

"I suppose not. Who told you anyway?"

"I don't know where it started. It's almost like an in-joke now." She sipped her tea and continued, "And in its own way it makes sense. I mean, you never told anyone at college you could shoot. If we hadn't come to Switzerland we'd never have found out."

"So? I hardly think a youthful interest in biathlon marks you out for being a hitman."

"It's not just that," she said defensively. "It's . . . I don't know, it's just so easy to believe I suppose. Of you anyway." The emphasis on the last three words knocked him slightly off balance, a glancing blow with its innocent suggestion that the deficiency had always been there, just like in a person marked for crime or serial killing or any other socially outcast trait.

"Why do you find it so easy to believe I could kill people?"

She laughed at the hurt quality of the question and said, "I don't know! Don't read too much into it. It's just . . ."

She seemed to catch up with her thoughts as she looked at him, her face freezing before she said in a more subdued tone, "Oh my God. It's true isn't it?" He could still easily persuade her otherwise, but it felt liberating somehow to be a simple admission away from her knowing. He'd come here to escape all of that for a few hours but now he wanted her to know. And he wanted to know, too, why it had been so easy for people to see him in that role, one he'd never even imagined for himself.

The question still hanging in the air, he looked at her and nodded, finally putting it into words. "It's true."

Though she'd guessed, she still looked stunned. "That's amazing," she said. And then, "You've actually killed people?"

"I wouldn't be a very good hitman if I hadn't."

"But when? How recently?" There was probably only so much honesty she could stomach, and the six in the last two days had been personal business anyway, so thinking back to the last proper job and embellishing it, he said, "Er, let me see, just over a month ago. I can't tell you where but it wasn't in this country. It was someone involved in the arms trade, someone who was threatening British interests."

"So you're like a soldier?" she said, falling for the spin he'd put on it. "Is it dangerous?"

"Not really."

"Do you carry a gun?" He nodded in response. "Even now, here?" Another nod. "Can I see it?"

"Do you want to?" He was puzzled by the request, something he might have expected from a male friend and which he'd have refused because of that. Coming from her though, it was different and when she confirmed that she wanted to he took it from the holster and laid it on the table between them, the silencer pointing away into the corner.

She stared at the gun without saying anything, transfixed, as if she couldn't quite believe it was there. She reached out and touched it lightly, once again as if to prove it was real.

"Do you want to hold it?" She shook her head and he said, "Shall I put it back?"

"I think so."

He slipped the gun back beneath his jacket and said, "Why isn't it surprising that I'm a hitman? I'm curious that other people saw it in me when I never saw it in myself."

"It's funny but I don't see it either now. You know, when it was some abstract idea it seemed to make sense." Her eyes looked elsewhere, like the gun was still on the table between them. "This is real though, not some fantasy of what JJ might be doing. I can't see it in you now, someone who kills people without even thinking about it, following orders; it's not who you are." She looked upset, and JJ already regretted that he'd told her; he didn't want her to think badly of him.

"That's just the trouble though—that's not who I am. See, I don't take orders as such, and I do think about it, and I do wonder how I—"

"How did you get into it?" she asked, preempting him, her mind on a rush.

"In a roundabout way I was recruited, that's all I can say. And yes, initially I was drawn by the excitement, the intrigue." He laughed. "Maybe I still am, I don't know. I have a nasty feeling I'd miss it."

"Does that bother you?"

"I don't know," he said, and then, "I have a good life, I have a nice place in Geneva, plenty of money, plenty of free time. I'm okay, you know, and I'm sure a lot of people who graduated with us have had a raw deal."

"What's the *but*?" He looked at her puzzled, and Jools smiled back at him. "You know, 'I have a great life, great house, de-dum, de-dum, de-dum, but . . .' So what's the *but*?"

He smiled too now and said, "Ah, *that but*." He thought about it, something he'd thought about plenty of times but had never put into words before. "Well, I don't know. Just that, sometimes I feel I've fucked up I suppose, big time. Fucked up in a way that's . . . I don't know . . ."

"But you're still young," she said emphatically. "You could retire, change careers, do something that lets you live the way you want to." She wanted him to do it, he could tell, one meeting in nearly ten years and she was desperate for him to give up, like he'd just admitted to a heroin habit or something like that.

He shook his head and said, "Trust me. That's not an option."

He'd seen a couple of people who'd taken that route of cutting themselves off completely from the past, had even killed one, but it was a sham existence anyway, a constant pretense that a history like that could just be folded away like a board game and forgotten about.

He smiled again, dismissively, and said, "You've caught me at a low point, Jools, that's all. I just need to find some balance, you know, to find some way of living a full life as well as doing this."

She smiled too and added, "Isn't that what we're all doing?" She patted her stomach to drive the point home.

He nodded agreement but thinking of her, of where her life was heading, lost in a future that seemed unavailable to him, he said, "That's a good point though, kids, stuff like that. Falling in love." He laughed, almost defensively, in response to the idea. "I really don't know if I could cope with falling in love."

"You haven't been in love since . . ." She didn't say the name, knowing that JJ didn't need her to, a sensitivity on her part even to the distant past.

"No, I don't think I have, which means I haven't I suppose. I've had relationships, happy ones too, but the thought of being in love with someone, being that close . . . It's scary, especially now." He felt like he was rambling, incoherent, his thoughts tumbling over the last day and a half, but it was obviously making some sense.

Jools suddenly looked concerned and said, "Are you in some kind of trouble? I mean, are you in danger?"

"No," he said quickly, making it implicit in his tone that the question was preposterous. "No, Jools, seriously. I don't have many chances to talk about these things, that's all it is, like I shouldn't really be talking to you, so it's just spilling out and not making sense. Really, I'm embarrassed to be going on about it, especially when there are so many other things we could be talking about." He did feel bad for burdening her, yet at the same time he'd wanted to tell her much more: that he was lonely, that he felt like indistinct bits of him were dying, that nothing was clear anymore. It was enough though, what he'd told her was enough, like a gasp of pure oxygen, burning the tissue of his lungs.

"I don't mind," she said, apparently reassured, taking it in her stride. "I'm glad you told me." And as an afterthought, "I suppose I have to keep it all very hush-hush?"

"I'd prefer it if you did. Tell them about my venture capital company."

She stared down into her mug, both hands wrapped around it as if for the warmth, and when she looked up again, she said, "So that's the real reason you've never been in touch."

It was as though the two things had only just found their way together in her head, and now, making that connection, she seemed happy that there had been a reason, that it hadn't been simply a case of him losing interest. Yet perhaps in truth, for a while at least, he had lost interest, the closeness he'd had with her and others seeming irrelevant.

"Maybe that's what I was trying to say before," he said, answering her. "It's difficult to balance things like regular friends, relationships, people who aren't in the know." Aurianne crashed suddenly through his vision, like a moth spinning recklessly into a lit room, hitting things at random, her smile, the way she undressed when she was tired, the scent of the shampoo she used. "It isn't fair on people," he said, shutting the memory off. "Even you, now; I'd never call you from my own apartment, never give you my number or address. I wouldn't want anyone to know that you know me. It wouldn't . . . it wouldn't be wise."

"That's scary," she said, shuddering slightly.

JJ jumped back in, quickly taking the edge off it. "Don't get me wrong, it's not a question of danger. It's . . . well, it's complicated. And, Jools, I can assure you, I haven't compromised you in any way by coming here. I'm very discreet, very careful, and I think too much of you, even if it has been eight years."

She smiled back and mouthed the words, "Me too," no sound coming out. The smile grew broader then and she said, "Why don't we open a bottle of Chilean red and we can sit and look through all my old photos and be really sad oldies?"

He nodded, smiling too, and saying as an afterthought, "Can you drink?"

"Glass or two now and again. Starting his or her education early."

"You don't know what it is?"

She shook her head in response and shrugged, like it was incidental knowledge.

They sat in the living room for an hour, drinking wine, looking through photos, JJ playing catch-up on various faces, Jools finding little to say about most of them, only that they were in some management job or other, that they were married, single, still with the same partner from college. They talked mainly about the past, the brief window of their student years, as though at graduation they'd stopped doing things worth committing to memory.

It was a good way to wallow out the evening, but as they

talked JJ could feel a sense slowly building inside him that maybe he'd come too far, even if some of the others hadn't. Maybe those friendships were only that, boxes of old photos, and there he was in some of them, but they were like pictures of a doppelgänger, someone who looked like him but had a different past, a different outlook, different DNA.

And as much as he enjoyed being with Jools again, as natural as it felt after just a couple of hours, what would there be beyond that? Even if he found some way of being in contact with her on a regular basis, what would there be to talk about except the child that would soon be her focal point?

Perhaps he would keep in touch in his own way now, dropping in once a year or so, out of the blue as he had that evening, so they could measure the progress of each other's lives for a couple of hours before parting again. And at some point perhaps she'd notice that it had been more than a year, two years, three, and that would be the mark of his passing in the world he'd once inhabited.

That was the most they'd be able to reclaim, never more than that, never even as much as the friendship they'd had before, all their conversations inevitably trapped in amber. He'd never be there for her, present tense, like other people would, and she'd only ever serve to remind him that all his potential for being someone else was locked into the past.

Later, as if she too sensed that this was a one-time thing, and wanting at least to prolong it for now, she said to him, "Do you want to stay over?"

"I can't, I've got an early flight out in the morning."

"Where to?" But she responded almost immediately to his expression, answering herself, "Oh. You can't say."

"Best not to." He looked at her then, sleep already wrapping itself around her like a blanket, seeing in her eyes though that she still wanted the company. "I can stay for a few hours if you want."

She even smiled sleepily. "That'd be nice. It's funny, but it's when I miss having someone."

It hadn't occurred to him that, as content as she seemed, she might still be lonely too, that his being there had perhaps taken the cold edge off her evening as much as it had his.

So they lay together in her bed, JJ helping her to prop pillows, making her comfortable, and he lay on his side with one arm draped over her and they talked to each other sparingly in the darkness, the words becoming fewer and fewer, the pauses longer.

When Jools fell asleep he eased onto his back, staring up at the ghost of the ceiling, thinking of nothing, then sinking unawares into the Bostridge hit, a stepped remembrance, descending into it till it was more real than the dark room around him. There was Bostridge slumped in blood, the girl captivating him, and that package, and that gaze as he stood in the elevator.

He was flicking through the wallet then, looking at the picture of Bostridge's family, trying to focus on them but seeing only blanked-out faces, and then he snapped out of it and was focused back on the room and Jools sleeping next to him. Thinking he'd slept too, he lifted his head and looked at her clock, reckoning from the time that only a few minutes had passed.

He'd lie there with her for another hour or so, get up and dress then, probably waking her a little. He'd kiss her goodbye in the darkness, not even rousing her completely, and by the next night it would seem dreamlike to her that he'd even been there.

And heading in the other direction, he'd be draping reality

over the bones of dreams, filling in those faces in Bostridge's wallet, finding out if somewhere in the shamanlike memory of that hit was the thing that had become his death warrant.

Perhaps he'd see the reality too, whether he wanted to or not, of the butterfly effect that resulted each time he pulled the trigger, the lives that spiraled away from those simple actions. It was a rare thing for someone in his position to see what death was, not in the instant but in the aftermath, where all its energies were absorbed. He didn't know whether he wanted to see it, but at the same time, somewhere hidden away inside him, it was there, pulling at him, scrambling his bearings.

9

By eleven he'd dealt with the mechanics of arriving in New York, picked up a few things, and still managed to get to the drab basement of Penn Station with over half an hour to spare. As always though, it had left him feeling like one of the walking wounded, and it wasn't even as if he could crash for the afternoon at his hotel, half the journey still ahead of him.

Instead he spent the afternoon and early evening on the train, winding in and out of the New England states, quite a few tourists among the other passengers, English accents audible here and there. He fit in with them too, dressed in casual clothes, his gun in a small rucksack.

It wasn't the private dead space of a hotel room but it wasn't too bad either, the relaxed rhythm of the train, its gentle murmurs. After lunch he catnapped on and off throughout the afternoon, ignorant of the aspiring autumn beyond the windows, hearing it though in the commentaries of other passengers.

He came around sharp just before six and looked out at the rural landscape, familiar, almost European, drenched in early-dusk light and shadow. It was a comfortable environment to be cocooned in, instantly recognizable but alien enough in the detail to feel like another world.

He'd bought a newspaper at the station and picked it up for the first time now, scanning through it like an Edwardian traveler looking for news from home. He scanned every headline, deciphering the runes, looking for some hidden hint in the news stories of what was going on. But there was nothing, no reports of car bombs, gas explosions, no snippets of unexplained murders.

Then he came across the one story he hadn't expected to find there, a short Associated Press piece with the barest facts on Dylan McGill, a twenty-year-old from Illinois, shot dead in Paris in a suspected street robbery. He'd been touring Europe before continuing his education. And that was all, AP leaving it to others to eulogize about American youth and turn over the ground for Pulitzers.

But there he was, the kid JJ had taken out, the only abstract indication to the outside world that something serious was happening in the shadows. He'd still have made the papers if JJ had left him there too, as the student from Illinois charged with the brutal sex murder of an antiques dealer, and how differently they'd have painted him then.

It couldn't have been down to chance that he'd been set up like that; he had to have upset somebody. And maybe he hadn't even been aware of it, just as somehow JJ had managed to cross Berg without knowing it, stumbling out of bad fortune only in that unplanned visit to Viner's, the same place where Dylan McGill had stumbled into it.

That was the way it was, always too much synchronicity,

like someone behind the scenes somewhere was mapping it all out for them, interwoven strands producing a pattern that was always just out of sight. The truth was though that there was no pattern, the connections were randomly generated, meaning nothing, possessed of no more significance than people chose to attach to them.

The connection he was heading into felt ominously significant, like he'd been heading toward it blindly for almost two years, but that too was a trick of his own mind, nothing more. It was only in his own mind that he was more than just a traveler, that they were more than a family that had suffered a loss, that their inn was more than a place for meeting a contact; it mattered only to him, the curse of carrying too much truth, too much knowledge.

But that didn't make it any easier, the thought that he'd be staying in their guesthouse, within breathing distance of their daily routines and of any hidden sadness. He'd have to meet that woman and speak to her, knowing what he knew, all the while playing the casual tourist. He'd probably see Bostridge's children too, the baggage of their loss perhaps even more easily visible.

Possibly Holden had chosen the Copley Inn for purely practical reasons, perhaps simply as somewhere Tom would know from his strange little riddle, a place with nowhere to swim. JJ couldn't help but think though that there must have been some satisfaction, whether Holden was in the business or not, in forcing him to go there, to face the people from whom he'd taken, knowing what they could never know.

If that had been Holden's intention it had worked well enough; the thought of it played on JJ's mind as he drove the final leg in darkness, a fine rain falling like a steady mist sprayed onto the windshield, the last half hour on back roads. His thoughts blanked again only when he saw the turning, clearly marked, on the near side of the small town where the inn was situated, the signboard knocking him into automatic.

Numbly, he climbed the couple of hundred yards up to the house, gravel crackling under the tires, trees mossy damp, and then the white clapboard expanse of the building, the porch lit, a few other cars parked around to the side. The rain was still falling, almost invisible but cool in his face as he walked from the car, bracing himself.

The main door was locked, the glass window in it looking onto an entrance hall with a large staircase. When he rang the bell a woman appeared, mousy hair, slim and attractive, casually dressed but stylish, expensive clothes. She looked in her mid-forties perhaps, old enough to be Susan Bostridge. As she saw him through the glass she smiled, opening the door then and saying, "You must be Mr. Hoffman." It wasn't the woman he'd spoken to on the phone; this voice was softer, younger.

"William Hoffman, yes."

"I'm Susan Bostridge." She reached out her hand and shook his. JJ was suddenly speechless, his mind tailspun by the mention of her name, the eye contact, the physical presence, this attractive pleasant woman whose husband he'd killed. But she distracted him then by looking at his sweater. "Oh, it's raining," she said and lightly brushed the fine droplets of water from his shoulders, an immediate comfortable domesticity that brought him around, putting him at ease. It wasn't what he'd expected, bringing him back to the moment.

"Idiots' rain," he answered her, smiling. "It's what the Turks call it."

"Idiots' rain," she repeated, the words hanging there for a second. "Have you driven up from Boston?"

"No, I came up from New York on the *Vermonter*, hired a car at the station."

"Oh, well that's a nice journey. But you must be tired! Would you like something to eat?"

He was already forgetting who she was now, the connection almost disappearing. "No, thanks, I am tired. I think I'll make it an early night."

"Then I'll show you to your room," she said, smiling, as much with her eyes as anything, a smile that looked for an old friend, like the loaded smile Jools had given him the night before.

He almost felt like he knew her too, and not for the obvious reason; her soft patrician voice and easy warmth disarmed him, making it all but impossible to associate her in his thoughts now with the pathetic figure of Bostridge and his child prostitute.

But being in her company even briefly was enough to make him think that memory might be unfair too. This was the man's wife, his home, a man who had to have had volumes more to him than the few tawdry Technicolor snapshots JJ had stored away. What did he know anyway of a man he'd seen only in a final moment of weakness and exposure? What did he know about any of them?

She talked him through the details of the place as she showed him upstairs in what looked to him like a typical American house, lots of space but willfully harking back to some indistinct past. Within a few minutes she'd left him in the homely clutter of his room, no ceremony, an offer still hanging in the air that he could have his breakfast as late as he liked, and that was it, the imagined significance of their meeting lost in the informal detail.

He sat there then with the world hushed around him, a deep peace that was almost unsettling, like no one else was there in the inn, like the fine mist of idiots' rain had smothered everything beyond. And it quickly began to work on him too, a calming blanket to set against the meatless sleep of the previous days, a secure comfortable peace in which to recover his senses.

He slept and no dreams came to him, his mind sinking into emptiness, the night devoid of shocks, of the heaving fishhook pulls on his heart, like lines tautening sharply against distant catches. He left himself at ease, becalmed, here of all places.

It was something he thought of when he woke the next morning, the strangeness of finding such peace in this house, a restorative sleep, a feeling that he'd slept for as many days as he'd been awake beforehand. It was completely at odds with the unease he'd had about coming here, this air of benignity around everything, from the first meeting with Susan Bostridge to the room he found himself in, filter-lit by the sun through chintzy curtains, as quiet as it had been the night before.

He checked his watch and saw that despite the offer he was in good time for breakfast, the perfect opportunity to break cover with Holden. Despite the restful atmosphere, he needed to know quickly what Holden could do for him, and what he wanted JJ to do in return; he wasn't intending to hang around on someone else's territory if there was nothing in it for him.

There were about a dozen guests at the inn, most of them sitting around a long table when he got to the breakfast room, two young couples, the rest middle-aged. They responded to the sight of him with a communal hello as if they were used to him coming in at that time, and an older woman serving them put down the coffeepot in her hand and said, "Ah, Mr. Hoffman, did you sleep well?"

"Yes thanks," he replied, recognizing her voice as that of the woman he'd spoken to on the phone.

"Good. Now why don't you sit right here and I'll introduce you to everyone?" He took the seat she offered him at the head of the table and went along with the strangely chummy ritual of being introduced, each couple responding like he was someone marrying into the family. They were all American but at the end the woman said, "You've missed our Scottish guests, the McCowans, already out walking, and of course Mr. Lassiter had to leave yesterday. But I think that's everyone."

One of the younger men up the table said, "Except you, Kathryn." His partner smiled approvingly at him, a couple not long together.

She responded as though to a bout of forgetfulness. "Of course, what am I thinking of? I'm Kathryn and this is William Hoffman. You like to be called William?"

"Actually, friends call me JJ."

Nods of acknowledgment were given around the table, people discreetly carrying on their conversations then as Kathryn said, "Now what can I get you for breakfast, JJ?"

"I don't really eat breakfast," he said apologetically, adding, "Just some tea please, if you don't mind."

"Oh but you have to eat something," she countered like it was an undeniable truth. "How about some blueberry pancakes? Once you've tried them there's no turning back." He gave in, accepting the offer rather than being cajoled into it like someone spoiling the party, and she went off into the kitchen looking pleased with herself. Another convert.

The couple to either side looked at him and smiled. The

man, introduced as Steve, looked like an off-duty mobster: balding, a solid neck that looked as wide as his head, a body that seemed to keep him away from the table.

He flicked his eyebrows in the direction of the disappearing Kathryn and said, "I never eat breakfast, only when I'm here. Any other time I'm in the office at eight-thirty, nothing but coffee."

His wife smiled benevolently and said, "As you can see, he makes up for it in lunches." Steve shrugged in response, a New Yorker's shrug, like there was nothing he could do about it so no point worrying. JJ smiled, unused to this kind of thing but going along with it, not wanting to stand out from the happy crowd.

They kept talking to him then, Steve the mobster turning out to be a lawyer, talking about the Copley Inn, about their grown-up kids, about the state of America, the last subject bringing agreement from people farther up the table. JJ listened for the most part, giving away only that he worked in venture capital, that he lived in Switzerland, that a friend had recommended the Copley.

He ate the breakfast, not finding it as addictive as they'd suggested but washing it down with the tea and feeling satisfied for having eaten it. Conversation continued to drift around the table, always genial, a general surge of goodwill each time a couple finished and left the room.

JJ let it all wash over him, but at the same time he was already turning over why Holden wasn't there, and why no one had mentioned him in passing. The absent McCowans received another mention, as did the apparently somber Lassiter who'd made room for JJ. Susan Bostridge got a couple of mentions, one woman dropping in that the children were beautiful, an all-encompassing, meaningless use of the word that nevertheless earned general approval around the table.

But there was no mention of Holden. It crossed his mind briefly that Tom Furst had gotten the location wrong, then that someone had already gotten to Holden, then perhaps that he'd given up on JJ coming and moved on. Whatever the explanation, he didn't seem to be there, and if Holden wasn't around there was no reason for JJ to be there either, no reason for him even to have made the trip.

On the other hand though, there weren't many further options that sprang to mind, apart from going to ground which in a sense he'd already done. And of course it was possible that Holden was there but keeping a low profile, staying in the family's own quarters, too much of a shadow to feature in the breakfast table conversation but there all the same and already aware of JJ's arrival.

At the end of breakfast there was one couple left at the table with him, Lenny and Dee Kaplan, well-preserved and perma-tanned, from some town in Southern California, a quiet sporty affluence about them.

When JJ asked whether they'd been there before Lenny said, "First time here in the Copley Inn."

"Not the last," added his wife.

"Definitely not the last. But we come to the East Coast every year around this time. It's our way of making our children love us." JJ smiled affably, seeing a joke coming; Dee was already holding back a giggle. "See, the grandparents move in to keep an eye on them; one week of that and they thank God they've got us for the other fifty-one."

"Isn't he terrible?" asked Dee. "Our two boys are great kids. I mean, really beautiful kids."

"It's true, I admit it," Lenny agreed, like it was never in doubt. Dee was the person who'd described the Bostridge kids as beautiful too, and as it turned out hers were around the same age. Lenny and Dee were eager to bring them the next time so the four could meet, no doubt in their minds that the Bostridge children would like their own.

A little while later Kathryn came through and said to the couple like it was their regular routine, "If you're ready to go in, I'll bring you some fresh coffee."

"Thanks, Kathryn, you're an angel," said Lenny, and then to JJ, "Join us? We always sit in the lounge and read the papers." JJ agreed, accepting Kathryn's offer of more tea.

The lounge was more like a sunroom, half conservatory, the Kaplans basking like lizards in the enhanced morning sunlight and warmth, as if needing a fix of their own climate. They didn't seem to read much but used the various stories instead as springboards for views on different subjects, stories about themselves.

At one point as Dee turned a page JJ caught a glimpse of a couple of columns and a picture of the kid from Viner's apartment, the kind of odd grinning portraits that he guessed came from high school yearbooks and always looked as though they'd been taken in the fifties. Dee focused on the story too, reading in silence for a few minutes before saying, "How terrible."

"What is it?" asked Lenny without looking up from his paper.

"This boy was traveling in Europe and they shot him. In Paris of all places." She looked at JJ and said, "Have you seen it?" He took the paper from her and looked at it briefly. The picture didn't do the kid justice, and didn't sum up either what had happened to him; JJ was thinking how a picture of his sleek corpse would have told more truth.

"I saw something about it yesterday," he said finally. "Paris can be a dangerous place."

"Isn't it terrible though? His poor family." Her words were

heartfelt, feverish with empathy, a mother with children approaching the same age where they'd go out into the world, fend for themselves.

JJ passed the paper to Lenny who'd looked up now. He looked at the article, or maybe just at the picture, shaking his head. "It doesn't make sense," he said, exasperated. "Kid goes on vacation and gets shot. In Europe, for God's sake." He looked at JJ then and said, "Maybe it wasn't a robbery. You know, maybe there's something we don't know about. I mean, why would they kill him? This isn't L.A. we're talking about, it's Paris. France, for God's sake! So why would they kill him, shoot him dead, just for a street robbery?"

It was funny the way he'd come close to the truth in his need for reassurance that Paris and Europe and life in general were safer than that; funny too how shocked he'd have been at the real, increasingly pointless reason for the kid's death.

JJ thought of him briefly, Dylan McGill, whose name he hadn't known, of the way he'd looked in the first few moments after seeing JJ, like he was involved in some practical joke. And he thought of his family and friends asking the same exasperated questions Lenny and Dee were asking, and of the new Dylan McGill they were building between themselves.

It was like they all wanted the fundamental truth of why it had happened, of why life was like that, but there were no explanations, at least not the explanations people wanted to hear. How much would it comfort them to know that their son, brother, friend had been killed as a precautionary measure by a hitman who only moments before had sought to help him? What use was that to anyone?

And as if to back him up in his reasoning Susan Bostridge

suddenly appeared, carrying a cup of coffee, and walked over to them, relaxed, graceful, like a model or ballet dancer who'd kept it into middle age. Whatever wondering she'd done about her husband's death it looked long stored away now; she looked at peace with life, content.

"Mind if I join you?" They all responded quickly and she sat down, turning to JJ then. "How did you sleep?"

"Very well, thank you."

"You look much better," she said like she'd been concerned by his appearance the night before, like he'd been ill but was on the mend. Turning to Dee, she asked, "Any news?"

"We were just talking about that poor boy who was killed in Paris," Dee said as though it was someone they'd all known.

"I saw it. Very sad."

"I still maintain," cut in Lenny, "that people don't get shot places like that for no good reason. There had to be something." Before he could expand on it again his wife threw him a glance and he crashed to a stop, looking sheepishly at Susan Bostridge then. "Me and my big mouth. Susan . . ."

"Don't be ridiculous, Lenny," she said, smiling, unperturbed. "And I know what you mean because it's a puzzle, it really is. But the sad truth of life today, anywhere in the world, is that people are killed for the most absurd reasons. None of us are immune."

JJ looked on nonplussed, an expression that concealed the uneasy sensation of being the killer of both the people they were talking about.

Having put Lenny at ease again, Susan turned to him and said, "I should explain, JJ. David, my husband, was killed two years ago in Moscow."

"Oh, I'm sorry."

"Just another Western businessman killed by the Russian Mafia. It got less press coverage than this poor boy and maybe that's as it should be." She wasn't dismissing her husband's death, her tone touched lightly with sadness. Inexplicably though, at the same time he got the feeling she hadn't loved him when he'd died, something in her face that was centered somewhere beyond having come to terms with it, like his death had merely tied up the loose threads of a separation that had already been completed in the heart.

And for the first time it made him wonder about the condom too. Bostridge had been wearing a condom and it made him wonder whether she'd been told about it, what she'd made of it if she had. It had never occurred to him before then how strange it was, that a dead man should be found wearing a condom that hadn't served its purpose.

It was such a minor detail, but if she'd been told it would have opened up all kinds of speculation in her mind: that he'd been unfaithful to her, that a girl had been there at the time of the murder, had perhaps even been involved. Equally though, with a Western businessman in Moscow, it was a detail even the police could have overlooked, so possibly she never had been told.

When he tuned back into the conversation Lenny and Dee were outlining their itinerary for the day, Susan showing interest in a list of tourist spots she'd probably heard repeated and described thousands of times before. She turned to him then and said, "And what about you, JJ?"

"I'm not sure," he said, suddenly on the spot. "I'm here to relax so I don't really have any plans. I suppose I'll have a look around, go for a walk." She looked enchanted by his lack of ideas, as if she was used to people treating their few days there like a military exercise.

"The village should keep you busy for an hour or so. And the woods of course; there are plenty of marked trails. And if you don't mind driving—"

"No," he cut in, "I don't want to drive anywhere today." He wanted to stay around the place, eager to spot Holden if he was there or to let Holden find him before the frustration began to set in. "I might try the woodland walks."

She nodded thoughtfully and said, "I'll join you if you'd like the company? Give you some pointers." She smiled before adding, "No extra charge."

"I'd like that, as long as I'm not keeping you from anything." She smiled again warmly. Lenny and Dee looked on slightly astounded, as though they couldn't quite work out how the new guest had so easily developed an unspoken rapport with their host, something they'd probably been working at assiduously for the full week of their stay, trying to belong.

There was a rapport too, like a tacit recognition that they were the same kind of people. Yet whatever similarities lay beneath the surface, whatever commonality there was in their backgrounds, he doubted somehow that they shared the same values, the same beliefs, that they felt the same way about life. Either way, it already seemed hard to believe this was a woman he'd dreaded meeting.

She was easy enough company too as they walked through the camouflage warmth of the woods, Susan pointing out the landmarks, explaining how the leaves would peak in a few weeks. Occasionally tourists passed them and strained to hear what she was saying, apparently recognizing a voice with some authority.

At one point they reached the top of a short climb and, turning, she pointed back down to where one end of the inn was visible between the trees; a couple of other buildings and a white church steeple were apparent farther on—the hotel was closer to the village than he'd thought at first.

"Beautiful, don't you think?" she said as they stood there. "Sometimes I think we're the luckiest people in the world to be living here."

Sometimes, he noted, only sometimes, when the world didn't intrude perhaps, and asked her then, "How long have you been here?"

"Since we married, nearly twenty years. The house was always too big for us but I fell in love with it at first sight. I like that it's an inn now." He glanced at her quickly, gauging the way she was thinking. She looked smitten with the place, even after all that time.

"Did you turn it into an inn when your husband died?"

"No, no, six years ago," she said. "The kids were getting bigger, David was often away on business, and I wanted to do something with myself, you know? Then one day I just saw it, saw how beautiful it would be as an inn and how I could share it with people. It became my dream." She turned to him. "And I've never looked back. I like being an innkeeper."

"I can see that," he said, smiling, and she laughed a little like he'd seen through her, that she was playacting, living a childhood fantasy like those children who dreamt of owning toy shops or candy stores.

They didn't mention her husband again; JJ was eager not to seem too inquisitive. Instead he asked questions about the running of the inn, keeping her on a subject she enjoyed, hoping that in the process she might mention Holden, the close family friend he still hoped was simply failing to show on the radar screens but was there nonetheless.

Once again he got nothing, and he was already beginning to think how he might proceed if Holden didn't show at all.

It wasn't as if he had many choices but one obvious possibility was to go down to Yale, to look for signs of him there or signs of where he might be; another was simply to give it up and get out of there.

But there was still time yet, and if Susan knew about Holden's background and knew he was in a fix, that would even explain why she hadn't mentioned him, particularly to a man on his own with no defined reason for being there beyond relaxing between business trips.

He didn't get the impression she was suspicious of him, particularly since she was out walking with him but, still stung from the way Esther had deceived him, he decided to test the water, saying when he had the opportunity, "The other people at breakfast seemed lukewarm about the chap who was here before me."

"Mr. Lassiter? Really?" It was a token effort not to be seen criticizing a guest but she gave up almost instantly, adding, "He was a little odd. Only about your age, said he was here on business but didn't say where or what he was doing. As a matter of fact he gave me the creeps; I think the other guests picked up on it too. Why, of course they did. They seem to have taken to you though."

"Good, I'm glad."

"So am I. I pride myself on having a happy atmosphere among the guests." She walked a few paces in silence and then said like an afterthought, "He'd come up from Washington. Wore a suit too."

He wondered if she'd turned the tables and was testing him now so he deflected it by saying, "A spy perhaps, on important business."

"Exactly," she said, laughing. "An ice cream spy! Not a very good one though. We're a long way from Ben and Jerry's." He had no idea what she was talking about but laughed anyway, guessing it was some tourist attraction, wanting to keep the light mood too, giving no indication that there was any more to him than met the eye.

When they got back to the inn he thanked her for the tour and went to his room, spending an hour or so doing nothing, a professional skill he'd developed, of shutting down and letting time pass, waiting. It was the final test; if Holden was there he'd definitely know JJ had arrived by now and would come for him.

Around lunchtime though he gave up, the frustration already beginning to wear on him, the fact that nothing was happening when it was meant to be. He walked down to the village, more like a small town as it turned out, well manicured, plenty of clapboard and picket fences and white-painted porches. It looked disturbingly familiar, a twilight zone quality dispelled only by a handful of awestruck tourists wandering around, some of them clutching jars of preserves or other wrapped gifts.

There were a few homely looking shops, a couple of restaurants, something calling itself the Old Maple Tavern which also proved to be a restaurant. Steve and his wife emerged satisfied as JJ neared it.

"Our secret's out," he shouted at JJ as he saw him.

"Good meal?"

"Red meat, guilty as charged."

His wife shrugged and said, "I'm telling you, the day he dies cows everywhere will celebrate."

"Yeah, yeah. JJ, what are your plans for tonight? I mean, if you're eating at the inn, well so are we. Karen and me, we'd be very happy if you joined us. If you want to, I mean, if you have no other plans?"

"That's very kind, thanks."

The lawyer and his wife both grinned, as though the two

of them had discussed the idea over lunch, and the three of them spoke on for a little while, tourist talk, their temporary location the only thing that linked them.

JJ left them and went into the tavern, ordering a chicken salad, what looked like the lightest meal on the menu. Other diners glanced over half sympathetically as he ate alone, the young waitress paying him more attention too, checking that everything was okay, asking where he was staying.

Far from being lonely though, the small talk with Steve and Karen and the dinner invitation had persuaded him to go down to Yale the next morning. For whatever reason Holden wasn't at the Copley, that seemed obvious now, and JJ didn't think he could stand the tourist camaraderie for more than a day, getting sucked gradually into being part of someone else's holiday. It wasn't something he was used to.

Susan Bostridge was more interesting, but that morning had been a one-time thing, he was certain of it, a welcoming gesture to someone who was on his own. And even then, most of what interested him about her was the link with her husband, a subject that was off the table, a subject it probably wasn't healthy for him to be curious about either, not when he was there.

It wasn't about fitting in or feeling comfortable anyway; he'd come there to get out from under a contract, to get Berg as Holden had implicitly promised. It didn't seem as urgent now that he was tucked away in Vermont, no longer a matter of pure survival like finding people in his apartment, but sooner or later it would catch up with him and become that urgent again. So whether he felt comfortable there or not he had to do something, either find Holden or rule him out and consider his moves.

The afternoon was pressing on by the time he got back to the inn. He could hear her voice as he walked into the lobby and went through to the dining room, where the large table was broken up into smaller units now. Susan was sitting on the edge of one of them talking to a stocky kid in his early teens, a bag slung over his shoulder.

They both looked in his direction as he stood there, the kid fair and good-looking but with a facial resemblance to his father that was unnerving, like a flashback.

"Sorry," said JJ quickly, "I'll catch you later."

"Not at all, JJ. I'd like you to meet my son."

He halted his bid for the door and walked over to them. "I just thought you might be busy."

"No," she said casually, "just chewing the fat after a day at school. This is Jackson."

"Jack," the kid cut in, good-humored but raising his eyes skyward.

"Hello, Jack. I'm JJ." He shook hands; Jack's grip was soft like it was a form of greeting he wasn't used to, though he probably got introduced to guests all the time judging by the breakfast-table conversation that morning. JJ turned to Susan then and said, "I just wanted to let you know, I'm going to New Haven tomorrow so I'll be leaving before breakfast, probably late back."

"New Haven? Yale?"

"Yeah." He left a slight breathing space, again giving her the chance to mention Holden, then added, "The daughter of a family friend's down there. I just found out she's going away the day after tomorrow so . . ." She nodded, almost as if she'd been expecting him to mention Holden too.

"We can arrange an early breakfast if you'd like."

"No, really. Thanks all the same." He smiled again, said, "See you around," to her son, and left, Susan asking Jack something else about school as they tailed out of JJ's earshot.

He went to his room then and studied the map, looking at the route down to New Haven. Holden almost certainly wasn't there either, not alive, but at least he'd be doing something, trying in some way to recapture the sense of momentum he'd had, the force that had carried him through Geneva and London, taking the bullet to them, letting Berg know that he was coming for them.

Of course, when it had come to the body count in London he hadn't achieved anything with that momentum, only a recognition of how little he could do on his own. Maybe he'd spooked them too, but that was only worthwhile if he could keep getting closer to them, and at the moment he couldn't even get to Holden.

But he had to do something, anything to move things on, realizing somewhere in that day's fabric that he had the wrong constitution for disappearing. Because that was what disappearing would mean, the life of a permanent tourist, soulless, drowning in small talk.

He couldn't die by degrees in a life like that, didn't think he could do it even for a few days, a revulsion that probably sprang from the same part of his character as the violence he'd come to live by. And maybe it wasn't much of a life but at least it was lived with eyes open, fixed on the common destination they all shared no matter what they did.

10

He spent a while walking around the university, relaxing after the long drive, soaking up the campus atmosphere. It was already hotter than the previous day and here and there people were sitting around on the grass, as many visitors as students by the look of it, the term probably not yet started.

He could understand why people like Holden were attracted to it, the academic life, another enclosed world, one step removed from reality and not quite as lethal either. Clearly though Holden hadn't been able to leave his old life behind completely; like Tom had said, he'd remained active, not finding enough to distract him in the stillness of art history.

When JJ saw a girl carrying a portfolio case he stopped her and asked directions to Holden's department, then made his way over there. His office was locked so JJ backtracked and found a secretary, asking her where he might find Holden.

"He's not in at all this week," she said, offering, "you could try his house."

"Okay, I'll do that. Do you have his address?"

"Well, yes, I do," she replied, suddenly cautious. "Could I ask why you want him?"

"Of course, though I don't need to see him for anything particular. He and my uncle are friends. My uncle said I should call in if I was down this way, which clearly I am, but I lost the piece of paper with the address and the only thing I could remember was that he taught history of art. Hopeless, I know."

"I see." She was already weakening, won over by his attempt at the affably inarticulate Englishman.

"But you're right you shouldn't give it. I shouldn't have asked in fact. Sorry. I'll check in the phone book."

"Oh you won't find it in there." She was smiling, writing down the address. She gave him the piece of paper then and said, "Now tell me where you're parked and I'll point you in the right direction."

The house was in an affluent suburb, leafy, wide open lawns. JJ pulled up outside the neighbor's house, went up, and rang the bell. After a couple of minutes a woman came to the door, probably only his own age but looking older, beginning to run to fat a little, her hair and clothes and whole demeanor lost in a comfortably premature middle age.

"Hello, is this Professor Holden's house?" She smiled like it was a mistake she was familiar with and pointed to the right. "Oh, I am sorry."

"Don't be," she said, adding then, "But Ed isn't there at the moment."

"Oh." He looked disappointed. "Do you know where he is?"

She shook her head with an expression of deep thought before she said, "But he must be away for some time because he has a house sitter."

"Oh," he said again, curious this time.

"European we think, but he doesn't speak much." Suddenly she glanced over his shoulder and said. "There he is now." JJ turned and saw a swarthy guy with cropped hair, in running shorts and a T-shirt, already breaking into a run as he reached the road. "It's the only time we see him. He runs every day, sometimes twice." JJ was still looking at him, lean but heavily built, not the kind of runner who'd be out pounding the road for hours.

"Well maybe I'll leave a note, or wait till he gets back. Thanks very much for your help."

"You're welcome," she said and disappeared back into the house. He got the feeling she'd be watching him from the window, nothing better to do with the long hours of the day, so he drove off up the street before parking again and walking back to Holden's house.

The runner was probably a Russian if they thought he was European, tying in with what Pearson had told him about Berg's connections. Only a Russian would be audacious enough, too, to move into Holden's house and carry on with his daily routine, not even hiding himself away. So he was almost certainly Russian, and if he was, that would be JJ's best lead so far as to what Berg was doing and where he was making alliances.

Once inside the house JJ moved around carefully, making no contact, doing enough only to check the rooms. There was a lot of ethnic decoration, African masks and figures, Asian prints. There was little to suggest anyone was living there, Holden probably absent for days, the Russian having

left no readily visible trace, no sign even in the kitchen that
anything had been eaten there.

He went upstairs, noting that the Russian was staying in
what appeared to be a guest room. There was a duffle bag in
the closet, most of his clothes still folded neatly inside it, a
couple of shirts hanging up, a suit. A smaller bag in the same
style was tucked under the bed, but JJ decided to check it after he'd dealt with the guy, not wanting to move anything the
Russian would recognize as having been moved.

He'd kill him first, then look in the bag. There wouldn't
be much point in interrogating him, not because he wouldn't
speak but because he wouldn't have much worth telling,
other than that he was there to kill Holden. And besides, re-
straining someone was always messier and harder than
killing him. He'd kill him, sticking to what he knew best, removing one more of the opposition, spooking them just a little more for what it was worth.

There were two bathrooms. Again, in one there was a
small shaving bag with his various toiletries still piled up inside it, a towel folded neatly over the one that was already on
the rail. It all gave the impression of someone with a military
background, overly methodical, no instinct, the kind of guy
who wouldn't sense the way most people could that there
was someone else in the house.

JJ checked the other upstairs rooms, settling finally in the
largest bedroom, the one he imagined to be Holden's, facing
the street, a large double bed, the same mix of ethnic carv-
ings and prints as elsewhere. Keeping away from the window
in case the returning runner saw him there, he did a quick
sweep of the room, finding nothing interesting, only a walk-
in closet that looked bare enough in places to suggest he'd
taken a lot of clothes with him.

Then JJ lifted the bedspread, checking if there was enough space under the bed for him to lie beneath it. At first it looked like there was nothing under there, but then his eye was caught by something, a flat package only just visible beneath it, something wrapped in cloth, perhaps nine inches by six.

His heart picked up a beat at the sight of it, a surge of memory, a jolt of anticipation as he pulled it out into the open, almost as if it were the same package. This was smaller than the one the girl had taken though, and solid, he realized as he unfolded the cloth that was wound a couple of times around it.

It was an icon, some saint or other in the Russian style, bathed in gold. As far as he knew they weren't particularly valuable but it was still a big market, and that probably answered the question of what Bostridge had been doing in Moscow, buying up stolen icons, a business Holden still appeared to be involved in.

That made the hit even more confusing though, the fact that JJ had been sent in by London to take out some black market art buyer. As he'd thought once before, Bostridge had to have had more business in Moscow than buying icons, because the Mafia might have killed someone who was only there on business but no one else would have done.

He folded the piece back into its cloth wrapping, thinking of the girl again as he did it. How transfixed he'd been by her that night and yet chances were she was already crumbling away from the beauty she'd had then, or dead, her capital used up, lives running faster out there than most places.

He'd thought of her often in the time since, her face popping up like a screen saver whenever his mind was idle enough. That night it had seemed like she'd had some wisdom to impart to him, her gaze containing truths about who he was, who they both were, but each subsequent time he'd thought of her she'd seemed more distant, less significant.

Now though it was like that night was fresh again, the sight and smell and feel of the package in front of him bringing back her scent, the way she'd looked, beautiful and naked, discreetly driven, and those eyes, an expression so intent it had turned him inside out. He remembered it all now, savoring the memory, the feel of it, an evocative triggering of the senses.

And then suddenly it was wiped out as he heard the front door open. He slid the package back under the bed, rolling under with it, pulling the gun from his bag, lying there in the dark with the smell of dust, the gun resting on the floor but pointing in the direction of the bedroom door. With his head low JJ would just be able to see his feet if he came into the room, and that would be enough.

The Russian stayed downstairs for a minute; there was the sound of water running in the kitchen, silence, the guy climbing the stairs, and silence again. He'd gone to his bedroom, but for a while there was nothing audible and it stayed like that until he went into the bathroom.

The shower started to flow. Then JJ heard him use the toilet and rested easier, a clear indication the guy still thought he was alone in the house. A moment later JJ heard him step into the shower, close the glass door behind him, the flow of water broken as it fell over his body.

JJ rolled back from under the bed and stood up, allowing himself a smile, thinking of showers, toilets, bedrooms—toilets probably the easiest, urinals in particular. Anything like that was a blessing, knowing that the victim was off guard, exposed.

The bathroom door was open and he could see straight away that the guy was just standing there in the shower with his back to him, not moving or soaping himself, just letting the water flow. It was a moment he could appreciate, the simple massaging pleasure of hot water after a run.

Confident that the guy was switched off JJ eased the glass door of the shower and stepped back again, letting it slowly swing open. It took a few seconds for the Russian to realize it had opened, and when he turned he still looked surprised to see someone there, like he'd been relaxed enough to believe that the door had opened on its own.

JJ put a bullet into his chest before he'd had a chance to register. He fell back heavily against the wall, sliding down it with a thumping splash, his legs flailing out of the shower's confines. He made no other sound, no moan or cry, no words, remaining mute against the gentle background sound of the shower.

He sat there rag doll style like he was drunk. He wasn't dead, and apart from the neat hole in his chest and the blood washing away with the falling water he still looked dangerous, muscular and taut, primed. His head was bowed though, a confused expression on his face, trying to comprehend what was happening.

Then, as if it had sunk in, he slowly looked up, produced a slight, disbelieving smile, and shook his head, acknowledging his own slip. Almost whispering he said in Russian, "Who are you?"

"No one," answered JJ. "Who do you work for?"

The Russian smiled again in response, the back of his head resting against the tiled wall now, the water falling down onto his upturned face. For a while he looked hypnotized by it.

JJ pushed his sleeve up and reached into the shower to turn it off. He went back into the other room then and emptied the small bag onto the bed alongside the Russian's discarded running clothes, the smell of sweat already turning stale.

The bag contained a couple of guns, ammunition, a mobile phone, two passports, one Russian and one Israeli, a wallet. The phone yielded nothing. He picked up the wallet and looked through it: a picture of a plain girl, another of the Russian with a mongrel dog, a small piece of paper with a phone number written on it.

At first the number looked familiar, and then he realized it was the first three digits, 802, the area code for Vermont. It meant the guy had a partner and the partner was somewhere in Vermont, which meant Holden was probably there after all, if not at the Copley then somewhere else.

The thought occurred to him then that the Russian had been Holden's man and that the contact number was for Holden himself. JJ dismissed it immediately though, certain that if Holden had run for cover he wouldn't have left someone at home with his forwarding address. He wouldn't have used a Russian either, not at a time like this.

But they were onto him; in one way or another Holden wasn't as safe as he'd hoped. Maybe he knew it too, maybe that was the reason he wasn't still with the Bostridges, whether for their sake or his own. And depending on the information the Russians had, the Copley Inn could be just as dangerous a place for JJ to be.

Even worse, as hard as it was to imagine, the entire comfortably domestic atmosphere of the place itself was in as much danger of being fractured by these people, and that of the family with it. That was Holden's problem, not his, but after just a day there JJ felt like he had a responsibility to eliminate that risk, at least for the time being, whether it served his own ends or not. And until he found Holden, it was best to assume their ends were the same anyway.

Either way, he had to go back up there, take the other Russian, try to flush out Holden in the respite. For the moment it felt like he was losing sight of the whole game, of who his real enemies were and how close he was. It seemed if he could only find Holden the pieces would begin to fall together again. He was aware more than ever that he was nothing without information, and that his information sources were dead or dried up.

JJ went down to the garage, checked out the freezer, then went back up to the bathroom. The Russian's eyes were still looking up at water that was no longer falling; he had the appearance now of someone who'd just crashed out of a race. JJ wrapped the larger towel around him, dragged him downstairs, and put him in the freezer.

When he left, he took the passports and phone number with him, and at the first pay phone he pulled over and called, getting through to an inn, asking where it was located. If he made good time he could maybe kill the other one before going back to the Copley, certain he'd rest easier knowing that the calm would be preserved, that no one would bring that violence back into the Bostridges' lives. It was the least he could do, to fend off for a while the thing he'd once delivered to them himself.

11

The Fallen Pine Inn was actually a roadside motel, low-rise, sprawling, like it wanted to be something else, a holiday village or something like that. As an opening gambit he called from the pay phone out front and was surprised when they happily answered his request for the Russian gentleman's room number, describing even where it was in the motel.

He went back and sat in the car for a while, with dusk beginning to dull the edges on everything, and he thought through the possible ways of dealing with the Russian. He had to kill him, that was certain, it was just a question of how and where.

The motel room itself was the easiest but didn't seem like a good idea. A Russian murdered in some city was one thing but JJ was in no doubt it would make big local news in Vermont, cause a lot of speculation. And though it was probably overcautious he couldn't help but think that kind of speculation would gravitate toward him, not least in the mind of Susan Bostridge.

So he'd get the Russian out of there, play on what he knew already to get the guy somewhere out of sight. He spent another ten minutes working it through in his mind, checking his map, then loosened the buckle on his small rucksack and strolled over to the far wing of the building, counting along the doors till he got to the right one.

He knocked and as he waited he savored the smell of the woods that surrounded the motel and the faint encroaching sounds as day shifted toward night. It was beautiful, even there. Then he heard the door opening, the security chain bracing itself across the narrow gap. The Russian's face was peering through; he had cropped fair hair, a military look like his partner.

JJ didn't smile but said matter-of-factly, "I'm Hooper. Berg sent me." The guy looked at him suspiciously, not like he didn't understand but like it still didn't explain JJ's presence. "We know where Holden is."

"Why are you here?" he asked, softly spoken, one of those Russian accents that was pitched halfway between mournful and musical.

"To show you where Holden is, and to help. He has two bodyguards." The guy still looked unconvinced but then JJ added like he was breaking bad news, "The CIA killed Korzhakov."

"When?" The Russian's eyes began to dance around a little.

"I don't know. Sometime today."

"I make a phone call," he said and JJ responded, blasé, "Okay, I'll wait." The guy left the chain on but didn't close the door, so JJ could see him as he walked across the room and was ready to make a move if he had to.

But the Russian checked his watch and didn't bother with the phone, obviously realizing that any place he wanted to phone was already in the middle of the night. Instead he put on a shoulder holster, put the gun he was carrying in it, disappeared from view, and appeared again at the door a minute later, wearing a suit jacket now and carrying a briefcase.

"Your car."

"Of course," JJ replied, making it clear that he understood the Russian's caution. He led him to the car, opening the passenger side first, throwing his own rucksack on the backseat to keep the guy relaxed.

Once they were driving he said to JJ, "You speak Russian?"

JJ glanced away from the road enough to shake his head. He'd already gotten the impression the guy's English was limited, so by pretending not to speak any Russian he could keep the conversation to a minimum.

Sure enough the Russian didn't speak again for a while. JJ drove a few miles more before turning onto a smaller road and turning again farther on, this time onto a single-lane track with passing points, the woods pressing up against each side, already darkening though the sky above was still blue.

After turning onto the track JJ said, "Holden's in a cabin, you know, for hunting?"

"Yes, I understand."

"He has two guards. CIA." He could see the other guy nod from the corner of his eye but could sense his caution stepping up a gear too, his eyes constantly scanning the road ahead of them.

At least until then it would have been a hard one for the

Russian to call. He'd been sitting it out in the middle of nowhere, not knowing where Holden was, waiting for information to come through, and then JJ had shown up pressing all the right buttons, giving no reason to suggest he wasn't on the level.

And if JJ had been there to hit him he'd have done it at the motel, not taken him to the woods to do it. JJ wasn't doing it for normal reasons though, and now it seemed that possibility was becoming real to the Russian. He kept his calm but said, "I think this partnership is good. You know Berg is very powerful man."

"More powerful now," said JJ.

"More powerful, yes. Together is much stronger." He paused for a second before adding, "You know Mikhail Sergeyevich?"

JJ shook his head and said, "I've heard a lot about him," kicking himself mentally as he said it, realizing how obvious it was for the Russian to throw up a false name.

He responded with silence, a couple of seconds only, but JJ could almost feel the Russian psyching himself up for the right moment. He'd blown it, was angry with himself, but when the Russian moved it was the wrong move, a twitch of the hand before going for his gun; a body blow first would have been smarter.

As he saw the movement JJ released the guy's seat belt and hit the brakes hard; old tricks always worked best. They weren't going fast, but the Russian slammed forward, his head hitting the dash, JJ feeling his own belt crunching against his chest. He released himself, giving the guy a hard drum-shuddering smack to the ear, pushing his hand under his body then and pulling the gun he'd been trying to reach for himself.

It took a couple of seconds, the guy not even finding time for an instinctive physical retaliation before realizing his own gun was pressing under the side of his jaw.

JJ was still catching his own breath but wasting no time he shouted, "Open the door!" He repeated it, pushing the gun hard into the guy until he did it, then shouted again, "Out, out," coaxing him with the barrel like before.

By the time JJ got out of the car the Russian was already running into the woods but he was disoriented and clumsy from the couple of blows he'd taken. JJ jogged after him through the bracken, almost catching him before the guy stumbled anyway, crashing down among the foliage, lost for a second in the gloom. Not realizing JJ was above him, he scrambled awkwardly to his feet, JJ waiting till he was halfway up before shoving him back onto his knees and pushing the gun into his face.

The guy was delirious, putting up no resistance now as JJ grabbed his face and forced the barrel into his mouth, the metal scraping and clattering against his teeth. JJ used the gun to lever his head back then, the guy squealing with realization in the moment before JJ pulled the trigger, the bullet kicking him away to the ground, the crack of the gunshot tearing a hole through the forest calm.

It took a few seconds for the sound to die away, the forest flooding back over it then and, a few moments later, the call of a bird in the distance, the sound harsh, menacing. Around him though there was an intense peacefulness, JJ not wanting to move for a while, wanting to remain there in the blanketing twilight, a druglike stupor in the smell and feel of the air, the violence of the last moments already lost.

Slowly coming back to himself, he wiped the gun, put it in the guy's hand, took a passport and wallet from his jacket pocket, and walked back to the car, cleaning himself up as best he could when he got there. Chances were no one would find the body for months, and even if it was days there'd be enough question marks to let it go as a probable suicide, a minor news story at most, easily ignored, no one at the inn ever guessing it might in some way have been connected with them.

Still conscious of how he'd look when he arrived back at the Copley, JJ stopped at a roadside diner, washed his hands and face in the rest room, drank an iced fruit tea. When he went back out to the car he picked up the briefcase, which he'd forgotten until then, lying on the floor in front of the passenger seat. He opened it, looked at the components snugly packed there, and smiled, strangely sentimental about the last time he'd used a rifle.

The remainder of the drive took no time at all, JJ getting back to the inn before nine. He stood for a minute when he got out of the car, a fresh-smelling stillness in the cool air, the porch and other lights behind him, a couple of smaller lights blinking in and out of visibility in the village, the top of the church steeple ghostly visible too against the dark blue sky.

JJ was lost again for a second, the whole world beautiful that night. He let it wash over him, snapping out of it only as a car turned up the drive toward the inn. He walked toward the porch but the driver of the car jumped out like he was in a hurry and reached the door at the same time.

"Hey," he said to JJ. It was a kid with a mess of black hair, quality slacker's clothes, a look that reminded JJ a little of Dylan McGill, a fresher, cleaner-cut version, or maybe just younger. JJ gave him a hello in response, and the kid stood back to let him walk through the door first.

Inside, a member of staff came into the lobby, a woman he didn't recognize but who still said, "Good evening, Mr. Hoffman. Did you have a pleasant trip?" He responded as quickly as he could and started up the stairs. She moved on to the kid then. "Hi, Freddie. I'll call Jem for you."

"No, I'll . . . ." the kid started hesitantly, his tone polite.

"Oh, here she is now." A girl appeared in jeans and a sweater, socks but no shoes, immediately, effortlessly attractive. She smiled at the woman who disappeared back toward the dining room.

She was so clearly Susan Bostridge's daughter, beautiful like her but with long mousy hair, as much like her mother as the son was like his father. There seemed something else though, maybe just because she was young, fifteen, sixteen perhaps, an extra quality that made it difficult for him to take his eyes off her as he climbed the stairs. He almost wanted to stop, to go back and introduce himself, to find out exactly who she was, what she was like.

As if aware of his gaze she suddenly looked up and for a moment met it with her own eyes, a brief, puzzled, searching look, a piercing intensity, almost as if she knew him from somewhere, recognized him, her pretty face lost in looking at him. He smiled, a meaningless friendly smile, and turned away, conscious suddenly of where he'd come from, feeling bloodied as if the signs of that last killing were all over him. He continued the rest of the flight without looking back, though he wanted to, and still with a hypersensitive awareness of her presence.

"Hey," he heard her say, and the kid responded with the same before her soft voice was there again, barely breaking cover. "So, you wanna come in?"

When JJ got to his room he put the briefcase and his own

rucksack in the bottom of the closet, took his boots off, and fell onto the bed, lying there looking up at the ceiling, his chest still tight and sore from the impact of the seat belt when he'd braked. As on the first night it felt and sounded like there was no one else in the building.

There were other people though, the girl and her boyfriend among them. He couldn't help but think of her, Jem, a girl who had to be about the same age as the one Bostridge had been with. That thought distracted him temporarily, how sick it made Bostridge, but he almost understood him too.

He felt snagged by the girl he'd just seen, a girl who was too young for him to be interested in, but snagged all the same, an immediate subliminal attraction like static in the blood, more than just the pull of youth and fresh beauty. Maybe she'd sensed it too in that moment she'd looked at him, knowing that she belonged with her boyfriend but sensing it all the same, two of those paths that should have crossed in a different time and place.

But then perhaps he was fooling himself, a beautiful teenage girl probably seeing him as just another guest at the inn. And it struck him that perhaps the way he felt now was the way it had been for Bostridge two years before, drawn despite himself, the Russian girl probably not even needing to approach him, just sitting in the bar nearby until Bostridge had lost himself in the possibilities and persuaded himself to talk to her.

He must have found it hard to believe his luck that night, that this descended angel had been willing to indulge him, his advances gradually stepping up and always accepted, too far in by the time she'd mentioned money. He'd never have realized that he'd been the one being seduced, and never realized either that the end had never been in doubt.

At least this was different in that respect, because JJ wouldn't be tempted, and because Jem Bostridge had no idea who he was, no reason to encourage him, even to speak to him. He was still drawn to her though, drawn in a way he couldn't explain.

He got up and looked in the mirror, checking again that there were no telltale signs he'd missed, and then there was a knock on the door. Still edgy after his day, he took his gun and held it out of sight as he opened the door.

A man was standing there, short gray hair, probably in his fifties but with signs of a physique, dressed like he'd spent the day hiking. At first glance JJ assumed for some reason that he was the Scottish guest he hadn't met yet, McCowan, but when the guy spoke it was an American accent, the voice instantly familiar.

"Sorry I missed you the other day. Ed Holden." JJ nodded, momentarily stuck for a response, and let him in. He put the gun away then and the two of them sat down in the chairs by the window. "Helen just came in and told Susan you'd come back looking tired, so, first opportunity."

"Where have you been?"

"I have a cabin up on Lake Champlain. I went up there for a couple of days." JJ laughed in disbelief, that the story he'd spun the Russian had been so close to the truth. "I should explain," continued Holden. "I thought it would take a few days before you showed up here and, though I'm sure it's not an issue, I didn't want to hang around the inn unnecessarily, just in case anyone stumbled upon me by accident." He waited for JJ to respond, but when nothing came he threw the original question back at him. "So where have you been? Susan mentioned Yale."

"Killing Russians."

"Not at random I hope," Holden said, smiling, "Yale has a lot of overseas students."

"I killed the one who was staying in your house, put him in the freezer. The other one was in a motel about ten, fifteen miles from here. Took him out in the woods."

Holden's smile slipped at the mention of the second Russian, the realization that they'd been closer to him than he'd imagined and that, however incomplete, they were getting information from somewhere.

He found another smile though, and said, "Well you certainly don't hang around." He seemed a lot more relaxed than he had on the phone, possibly just because the forced awkwardness of the satellite had made him seem more tense than he'd actually been.

"Nor do they," said JJ. "And speaking of which, I hope you realize how lucky you were to catch me the other day."

"Oh I do, though persistence played a bigger part than luck. Anyway, I didn't call you because you were the only person who could help me, and that's not to deny your undoubted skills. On the contrary, I called you because I felt a sense of obligation. You see, in effect, it's my fault you're a target." He wanted JJ to ask why, a breezy playfulness about the guy, like it was all a joke.

"I don't go for riddles," JJ said, getting another smile out of Holden, like everything JJ said reminded him of himself when he was younger or someone else he'd known.

"I'll explain everything tomorrow but I shouldn't stay any longer now." He sat forward on his chair, ready to get up. "Have your tea in the lounge after breakfast. We'll meet by accident, take a walk."

"Susan has no idea about me."

"Absolutely not. But she's okay with the business." He looked deep in thought for a second and added, "After our walk, I'll reveal that we have a common friend in Tom Furst. It'll make it easier, you know, the transition from guest to whatever."

JJ didn't see why he needed to make that transition, wasn't certain even that he wanted to. There was curiosity of course, that same lure of being allowed briefly through a door, from his side of death to theirs, but that still seemed an unhealthy curiosity to indulge.

And no less unhealthy was the curiosity he'd developed without warning in the last half hour, something that was fusing itself more and more in his head with the girl of two years before, even though there was no resemblance, though they had nothing in common. Almost nothing.

As if sensing his disquiet, Holden stood and said cheerily, "So how does it feel, being here?"

"I don't know," answered JJ truthfully. "I was uneasy about coming here, obviously, but now I'm here, I don't know, I don't feel anything. They're just people."

Holden nodded, not smiling this time but looking like he understood. "Isn't that what it's about, knowing when to feel and when not to? Thanks for the Russians by the way."

JJ smiled, warming to the guy's tone, and said, "You're welcome."

Holden walked over to the door and left. JJ got up and locked it behind him and then lay back on the bed, aware that he hadn't been entirely truthful, that he was beginning to feel something toward them, however hard it was to pin down.

He had a good feeling about Holden though, despite the initial reservations, the suspicion of a stranger who knew things about him. He'd withhold his judgment till he got the full story, but if it was true that Holden felt obliged to him, that in itself was rare, a person who felt obliged to anyone when his own spot was marked.

There was something else too, the way he'd thought about introducing him to the Bostridges as a friend of a friend. It seemed to tie in with the way Tom had spoken about him, leaving JJ wondering why he'd never heard of Holden before. But then he'd never needed to know who any of these people were before.

Just as, until then, the families of victims had been distant people, characters in stories whose lives and emotions he'd only imagined. And now he was almost in among them, perhaps only a day away from getting to know all of them, from being accepted as a friend. It was a strange prospect, but suddenly something he felt compelled toward, for the most questionable of reasons, because he'd seen that victim's daughter from the stairs and she was beautiful.

12

After breakfast he sat in the lounge again with Lenny and Dee, looking through the papers, the same superficial reflections. He didn't learn much more about them, other than the odd fact that Lenny owned aircraft hangars for a living.

They mentioned their boys just as much, a trait he found touching, the fact that even for one week in Vermont they clearly missed them. The prospect of bringing them along on the next trip rose again, JJ imagining how the boys would most likely become besotted with the Bostridge girl and all the emotional crises that would entail.

The first sign that Holden was coming was Kathryn bringing in a tray with a pot of coffee and a cup on it. She didn't say anything, just set down the tray and left, and a minute or two later Holden came in, picked up the tray, brought it over to join them.

"Another fine day," he said triumphantly, like he was talking about the stock market or the economy. "Mind if I join you?"

"Not at all, Ed," Dee replied, just as enthusiastic. "How was the lake?" Lenny looked up to hear what Ed had to say.

"Beautiful, beautiful. Something special." There was that look again, the deep-in-thought look JJ had seen the previous night, before he added, "You know, if you're back here next year, feel free to take a few days in the cabin. You're more than welcome."

"That's very kind," said Lenny, and Dee looked in danger of throwing her arms around him, like all their efforts had paid off, a sense of inclusion. "We might just take you up on that offer."

Ed smiled and nodded, a little embarrassed perhaps by the emotional pitch of their response. He turned to JJ then and said, "I'm sorry, we haven't met but I guess you're JJ. I'm Ed Holden."

They shook hands, JJ saying, "Pleased to meet you, Ed. I take it it's not your first time here?"

"No, in fact I'm not a guest. Old family friend. And you're here between business trips I'm told."

"That's right," said JJ. "Recharging the batteries."

Ed nodded and turned to Dee who was still looking on, Lenny having gone back to the papers. "So what do you two have planned for today?"

"Highlight of the trip," she said, rolling her eyes. "We're making the drive up to Ben and Jerry's!" It was the second time JJ had heard that; he remembered now that it was an ice-cream brand, guessing it was made somewhere nearby. As if to reinforce the fact, Dee asked, "Do you have Ben and Jerry's in England, JJ?"

"Yes, we do," he said, letting go that he'd already told them a couple of times that he lived in Switzerland.

Ed wagged his finger at her teasingly and said, "Just remember, a moment on the lips"—the three Americans finished the phrase together then, a summer camp chorus—"a lifetime on the hips!" That accomplished, Ed turned to JJ, asking, "And what about you, JJ, any plans for the day?"

"Just walking about the place, taking in the woods."

"That's what I'm planning for the morning. Maybe I could join you, if you don't mind the company?"

"Not at all." He noticed Lenny and Dee looking hoodwinked again, could imagine them trying to work out later why the English guy seemed to get taken so easily into the fold, consoling themselves perhaps with Ed's offer of the cabin.

When the two of them set off for their walk a little later, Ed pointed to a part of the garden that sloped down into a small hollow surrounded by trees.

"See there," he said. "When David and Susan first bought this place there was a swimming hole down there. So when Jem was born he decided it was dangerous and that he was gonna fill it in. One of the neighbors objected, said it would damage the wildlife, but no one could find anything in there, not so much as a frog. Then someone else came forward, said the hole was artificial anyway, dug by the people who had the place before the war, family called Timmins. So he started to fill it in, but the Timminses had chosen a good spot; it was two winters before he finally cracked it." They'd walk on a way but Ed stopped and turned back to look at it now, saying, "David did a good job too though, never seen it flooded since. No sign at all it was ever there."

"Nowhere to swim," said JJ, appreciating how smart it had been to use the phrase.

Ed nodded and said, "It's something of an in-joke among friends, 'specially people who've been here midsummer."

"It wouldn't have been Tom who gave away that you were in Vermont?"

"Absolutely not," Ed answered, leaving no room for doubt. "And if it had been Tom, I hardly think the Russian you dealt with would have been fifteen miles away."

"True. It's the way I am, though. I never rule anyone out." Yet once again the nagging doubt was there, the way he'd almost let Esther get to him. It had been an easy mistake in exceptional circumstances but there was never any excuse, and if Esther hadn't made mistakes too they'd have still been cleaning bits of his brains from the mosaic floor.

Holden knew nothing about it though, and just as JJ was mentally chastening himself for trusting someone he said, "That's the smartest way, but in the end it's the loneliest too. You have to have people you can trust, have to have an instinct for it. Like you, I trust you already, just as much as I trust Tom. I don't believe it would ever figure in your game plan to double-cross me. It's who you are."

JJ laughed a little, taking the compliment but not believing it for a minute. Holden was coming across as too laidback for someone who'd been in the business that long, JJ certain there were more layers than he'd ever see beneath that easygoing surface.

"Well I'm glad you trust me," he said. "Now why don't you tell me what's going on?"

Ed nodded but didn't say anything at first, waiting as two people passed them on mountain bikes, coming off the woodland trail they were just about to start up. Ed and the cyclists exchanged greetings, and then as they walked on he pointed vaguely at the tree canopies, saying, "In a few weeks there'll be people like that swarming all over these woods."

"Yeah, Susan told me. Leaf peepers."

"Leaf peepers," Ed repeated, apparently amused by the term. "So you want information."

"Well, as you just pointed out, I'm too early for the leaf-peeping season."

Ed laughed again in response, still smiling as he started to speak. "I still have something I need to figure out, but this is how it's shaping up. David and me went a long way back, similar backgrounds. We started a business venture buying art in Russia, selling it here, mainly for David—he liked the excitement." JJ smiled, thinking of how much excitement Bostridge had ended up getting, and as if thinking along the same lines Ed said, "Quite. The thing is, David was never a company man or anything, but he started to get involved with little bits of company business here and there, you know, like carrying messages, information. It was all a game to him, like being in a James Bond movie."

"It certainly has a familiar ring to it."

"It gets more familiar. A couple of years ago it seems David crossed some boundaries and it goes down that London wants him removed. Berg's pulling the strings and, cautious as ever, he decides to run it past me first. Not like I have a veto, just to keep everything sweet."

"You knew Bostridge was gonna be killed?"

Ed nodded and said, "From the first time he went to Moscow I knew he'd end up taking a bullet. It still came as a shock, 'specially that it was us doing the killing." He fell silent for a couple of paces, either trying to work something out or just lost in thought, pulling himself back after a moment or two. "So anyway, I wanted him to be taken down by someone decent, someone I knew would do it properly, quickly. I insisted on you or Lo Bello. Berg said he could get you. So that's why it's my fault you're involved, why I felt obliged to help."

JJ took in what he'd heard so far, intrigued by the mechanics behind what had seemed like a straightforward hit. "I'm following you," he said, "but I don't see where this is heading. You think Berg wants me dead because I unknowingly killed someone for him two years ago."

"He wants you dead," Ed said, clarifying the point, "because he can't be sure Viner never told you that it was Berg's hit. See, I made some inquiries afterwards and no one I spoke to knew how David had crossed the line. The more I looked, the more I began to think the hit was personal business for Berg, probably a favor for some gangster or other."

"And?"

"And now, for whatever reason, Berg wants to eliminate everyone who knew or might have known about the hit. There's been some ballast, but most of the key people targeted in the last couple of days were connected in some way with the hit on David. Of course, typically for Berg, he's been methodical about making it look like something else, but he's done this before. You have to hand it to him, he's a smart cookie."

"You have no idea why?" It was already looking obvious to JJ but he wanted to get as much as possible from Holden before he started speculating.

"I've got a lot of people looking into options for me, but nothing concrete, no."

They'd reached the point at the top of the climb that looked over the Copley and the village. Ed stopped to take it all in. "This is one of Susan's favorite spots," he said, taking a deep breath as if he could draw all of it in like that.

JJ looked at it too, nodding, in no real mood for scenery though, his mind stacking things up. It seemed hard to believe Holden wasn't ahead of him, but then Berg was probably better at fooling his own kind than he was anyone else, intelligence people always too eager to construct puzzles where there were none, looking into the distance when there were corpses at their feet.

"What about the Russians I killed? Doesn't that suggest the most obvious connection?"

"I don't think so," said Ed, his tone dismissive. "They'll have been Sarkisan's people. Berg and Sarkisan have been in bed together for years. And he wouldn't care about who killed David; it might even have been his call."

"I wouldn't be so sure about them being Sarkisan's men," said JJ. "Someone told me the other day that Berg's been making some high-level contacts *recently*, that they were taking care of his protection at the moment. So maybe it's those contacts he doesn't want finding out about Bostridge. I mean, Bostridge must have had some powerful friends out there if someone like Sarkisan didn't want to be seen to hit him."

Ed looked at him, impressed that JJ had come up with something he'd missed, like he'd never anticipated getting anything as ethereal as information from him, or a theory.

"Who told you this?"

"Stuart Pearson." There was a moment of calculation then on Ed's part, despite his claim of complete trust in JJ, and the careful question, "Pearson talked to you?"

"That's one way of putting it. I was threatening to kill his children at the time."

Ed smiled indulgently, relaxing again, like JJ was a student owning up to his part in a drunken prank. His face took on a different expression then, one of satisfaction that the simple piece of information from Pearson was all he'd needed to see what everything came down to. "Then I think you're right, we have an answer," he said, then digressed, "Did you retrieve anything from the two Russians?"

"Couple of passports from the house sitter, another from the tourist."

"Good. I'll go down to Washington with them tomorrow, make some inquiries. I'm pretty certain, though, that these links you're talking about must be with Naumenko. It all adds up, everything you've said."

Ed started walking again and after a few paces JJ said, "Aleksandr Naumenko. I've heard a bit about him."

"But not much," added Ed. "He's an interesting character, smarter than the rest put together, just as ruthless, discreet with it, and if he isn't the most powerful man in Russia already, he certainly will be. No one wants to touch him either. The other bosses all respect or fear him. Incredible." Ed looked in awe, like he was discussing some historic figure.

JJ thought instead about what it meant for Berg to have this person on his side, the obstacle of freeing himself and Holden from the contract suddenly looking insurmountable. In the light of it the last few days picking off people here and there seemed as much a game, as much a fantasy, as Bostridge acting the spy in Moscow. JJ said, "So do you want to share with me why this is good news?"

"Of course." Ed nodded, smiling. "You see, if it's Naumenko it does explain why Berg wants us dead, just like you said. Because we know that he killed David, and Naumenko loved David, I mean loved him, chemistry between them. Strange but there it was. They did a lot of business together, became great friends. Apparently he cried when he heard David had been killed. He never forgave me either, said I should have made David more aware of the dangers."

Ed looked lost again, like he blamed himself too. It made

JJ think back as well, to his own preoccupation that night, never realizing that somewhere, probably in the same city, a man as dangerous as Naumenko had been reduced to weeping over David Bostridge, and that back in America Holden had waited, knowing that the trip would end badly, that he'd have to comfort the family, knowing all the time that he'd sanctioned it, chosen the killer.

"So in theory," JJ said eventually, "if it is Naumenko, we only have to tell him what we know about Berg and that should give us some movement."

"Exactly," said Ed. "You just sit it out here for a day or two, I'll go down to Washington, and then we'll see what happens." They walked on a short way without speaking before Ed added like an afterthought, "A shame we couldn't have done something before they got to Larry."

"You knew Viner?" JJ asked, surprised.

"Yeah, pretty well; I always looked him up when I was in Paris. Actually I had lunch with him a couple of months ago. Fakhr el Dine, you know, at the IMA?"

"I know it. He used to lust after the waiters there."

"Yeah," Ed agreed, tacitly acknowledging the vast underbelly of Viner's life, a side of him that was only vaguely hinted at in his lusting after young waiters. "Yeah, he was a sick individual. And maybe the world's better off without him. He was decent though, where it counted." JJ nodded, not saying anything, and Ed said, treading carefully, "I heard about your girlfriend too."

Again, JJ nodded but said nothing, feeling there was nothing to say to someone who hadn't known her, or them as a couple. He felt too like he wanted to avoid any situation where someone might sympathize with him on Aurianne's behalf, sympathy that would have stuck in his throat, sickened him. Instead, he shifted the conversation back to Holden, saying, "You're not married yourself?"

Ed raised his eyebrows in response. "Fifteen years," he said, correcting JJ's assumption. "Jane's a professor at Yale too. Thankfully, she's visiting with her family in Sydney at the moment. But like Susan, she's okay with the business, you know? She understands the risks."

JJ reeled slightly, his shock based mainly on his impression of the house, a place which had looked like only one person lived there. He was certain too that the walk-in closet had contained only men's clothes, but maybe he'd been mistaken, or maybe the missing clothes had been hers rather than his.

"No kids?"

"No. We put it off and put it off and in the end it just seemed too late."

"And you don't find business messes your life up?"

"No," Ed said, matter-of-factly. "Until this came along. And that's the beauty of still having your hand in, knowing what's coming, getting tipped off." He looked at JJ then, saying, "You know, you're never gonna live a normal suburban commuter's life—and who'd want to? But you can find a balance, with the right people, the right mix of trust and caution. It can work. Life can be good." JJ smiled, bemused that Ed had so easily seen through him, like it was common for people of his age to be preoccupied with how they could square things up. "I'll tell you something else," added Ed. "I would never advise trying to cut your ties with the business, but you can do other things too."

"Become a professor." JJ laughed.

"You wouldn't be the first, or writer or journalist. There's no hurry, you're young, but there are futures."

"I'll bear it in mind," said JJ, still smiling but finding some comfort in the conversation, in Holden generally, the way he seemed to wear it all so lightly, like a man who'd come to terms with himself.

They walked on for another hour or more, Ed talking about his move into academia, about his career before that, a short spell in Vietnam, longer spells in Eastern Europe. They touched upon the subject of the Bostridges now and then too, almost in passing, and JJ found it reassuring to talk to someone who was as implicated in Bostridge's death as he was and yet who was able to separate that fact completely from his ongoing relationship with the family.

Eventually they came to the village from its far side and stopped for lunch in a small restaurant, one JJ hadn't even noticed on his previous walk, country-kitchen style, plenty of happily overweight couples eating in there. The waitress knew Ed and spoke a few words to him nearly every time she passed, Ed responding each time, his smile increasingly strained.

They'd finished eating when JJ remembered the icon from the previous day and said, "Found something under the bed yesterday, reminded me of something I saw in Moscow." He was careful not to mention Bostridge by name in such a small place.

The response was dramatic all the same, Ed asking urgently, "You know what happened to it?" His eyes were sharp and focused, like the mention of it had reawakened something he'd long given up. It was amazing to see, how the contents of the package stolen from Bostridge could electrify him like nothing else they'd talked about, the laid-back Holden completely shed.

"The girl took it," JJ said. "He was with a prostitute."

"David!" Realizing he'd spoken too loudly Ed lowered his voice as he added, "He would have run a mile from someone like that, believe me." JJ wondered if the original information on Bostridge had come from Holden and if perhaps he hadn't known his friend as well as he'd thought. Ed seemed to pick up the doubt in JJ's eyes and said, "I know what you're thinking, and I admit it, it's a shock to me that he was with anyone at all, but a hooker, absolutely no way."

"How about some coffee?" said the waitress, suddenly appearing at their table with a cheery smile.

Ed transformed himself immediately, smiling, giving a hint to JJ of how easily he adopted that look of having nothing to worry about. "That's a great idea, Megan. Coffee for me. Tea for my friend?"

"Yes, tea please," confirmed JJ. He'd spoken to her a few times, but she smiled now and said, "Over from England?" He smiled back, nodding, not saying anything though, not wanting to encourage the conversation. Once she'd gone he cut back to their own, picking up where Ed had finished. "I thought you said he had a taste for excitement?"

"He did but not in that department. And he was obsessed with disease." It made JJ think of the condom again, and of the girl who, if Holden was right, had done an incredible job in luring Bostridge astray. He was forgetting, though, that he'd seen her and that she probably hadn't needed to try particularly hard, maybe just sit in the bar like he'd imagined, her job even easier if she hadn't had to ask for money. It was compelling all the same, the slim possibility that she hadn't been a prostitute, or at least that she hadn't presented herself as one to Bostridge.

"Whatever she was," JJ said, voicing his thoughts, "she was in bed with him when I got there, and she took the package. She searched the room, found it under the bed. No, she looked under the bed straightaway, like she knew where it would be."

Ed looked shell-shocked, as much by the presence of the girl as by the loss of the package.

"I've often wondered what happened to it." He pulled himself back into business mode and said, "See, I didn't find out it would be on that trip till after David had left. So it was short notice, but I still made arrangements for the merchandise to be retrieved. When I was told it was missing, I assumed someone somewhere along the line had taken advantage of the situation, common enough out there, but I can tell you, it hurt more than usual on this occasion."

Again it was interesting to hear him talk about being hurt by the loss of a package when he hadn't used that kind of sentiment once in talking about David Bostridge. Perhaps it was because that kind of hurt was programmed into his system, or perhaps JJ had gotten him wrong, fooled by the flip exterior, and in truth it still hurt too much for him even to broach it, skipping across the story lightly instead, talking about swimming holes, Dartmouth, family backgrounds, anything superficial rather than deal with the intense and difficult truth at the heart of it all, the open wound of what he'd done.

"Won't be a second," the waitress informed them as she passed with two plates of food.

"Thanks, Megan."

"What was in the package anyway?"

"An icon," said Ed. "But no ordinary icon. It came from a church in Pechorsk, small town near Archangel. Probably came from Novgorod originally. The Annunciation painted on a wooden panel. The only icon in existence that we can say with some degree of certainty was painted by Theophanes. The ultimate prize, and a beautiful piece of art, truly beautiful!" He was fired up with describing it, offering a brief insight into how he probably was in the lecture hall.

It explained too why he'd reacted so excitedly to the mention of the package, perhaps even explained the girl's behavior that night in Bostridge's room. But then the girl, whatever she'd been, had almost certainly been following underworld instructions, driven not by the same reverence as Holden but by fear of what they'd have done to her had she failed to bring it back.

Suspecting then that even Holden's reaction had been as much about money as anything else, JJ said, "Was it valuable?"

"Too valuable to be lost," he said. "I don't mean the money either, though this was an exceptional piece in a modest market. For someone in my field, to have had a piece like that in my hands, even for a short time . . ." He trailed off and then Megan appeared, cluttering around the table, apologizing for the delay which she put down to the tea.

When she'd gone again JJ said, "It was stolen though?"

"Of course," said Ed, the question ridiculous. "But we had a buyer lined up, someone with an extensive, mostly legitimate collection. He'd have left it to a museum when he died. It would have stayed there until a suit was lodged for its return, by which time Russia would have stabilized enough to ensure the piece's safety. Sometimes stolen art is secured art, you know? I have no qualms about it."

"As long as it's stolen by the right person."

"Exactly," Ed said, acknowledging JJ's mocking tone with a smile. "But don't worry, that icon will resurface. I'll stake my career on it." JJ nodded, sipped at his tea, wondering idly which career he was talking about.

When they got back to the inn Ed insisted on introducing
JJ properly to Susan, leading him through a door in the hallway to the part of the building that was still their private
house. It was decorated much the same way as the main part
of the inn, given away only in the domestic detail, a pair of
training shoes on the floor, a jacket thrown over the banister
at the bottom of the stairs.

Ed led him through to the kitchen where he could already
hear Susan talking to Jack, the same catching-up conversation he'd walked in on before. JJ checked his watch then, surprised that he and Ed had been out for so long.

They were sitting either side of a kitchen table, strewn
with paperwork, drinks, a half-eaten sandwich in front of
Jack. Susan smiled at Ed as he appeared but kept on with
what she was saying to Jack, some question about a kid
who'd been in trouble, interrupting herself only when she
saw JJ.

"Why, hello, JJ," she said, smiling but looking surprised to
see him there, wondering perhaps why Ed had brought a
guest into their private space.

"Hello," he returned, nodding to Jack who'd looked over
to see who was there.

"Susan," said Ed, "I've been out with JJ today and it turns
out we're connected. JJ's a great friend of Tom's."

"Tom Furst? How amazing," she said, lighting up with the
news, and then to JJ, "You know, I sensed when you first
came that you were, I don't know, one of us I guess. What an
amazing coincidence!"

"Not really," he said sheepishly. "I didn't want to say
anything, but it was Tom who recommended this place."
She smiled, shaking her head in disbelief, her eyes full of
warmth. It was as if she had sensed a connection with JJ, as
if she'd wanted him to be more than a guest and was

pleased now because there he was, one of them by association.

"Well come and sit down," she said, clearing some of the papers into a pile, and then as they sat, one on each of the two remaining sides, "How about coffee? Or I can ask for tea? I make the most appalling tea." They both declined. Jack went back to his sandwich and a glass of strawberry milk that left his top lip with a mustache each time he drank from it. For a minute Susan looked like she didn't know where to begin but she said finally, "So are you actually in the same line of work as Tom?" There it was, a loaded question that had the capacity to open doors all the way to the facts of her husband's death. Remembering what Holden had said about her though, about being okay with the business, he said carefully, "In effect, yes I am."

"You're like, a spy?" asked Jack, wiping the comical pink mustache with the back of his hand. He looked vaguely interested in the idea, like it was a career he was considering, or possibly because that's what he thought his dad had been.

"Tom isn't even a spy," answered JJ, smiling. "And what I do is even less exciting than what Tom does." Jack looked at him, a skeptical expression on his face, as if to make clear to JJ that he knew more about these things than most kids his age.

"I still find it hard to believe Tom's a grown-up," Susan said.

Ed cut in, "Susan, your own kids are grown-ups. Look at this big guy here."

Jack raised his eyebrows and looked at Ed, spelling it out. "Ed, I'm like, fourteen, which is like, a kid. *You're* a grown-up!"

"Debatable point," Susan said, turning back to JJ with a

familiar American openness. "Why don't you join us for dinner tonight?"

"That's a great idea," said Ed, looking at JJ.

"I'd like that, thanks."

"Do I have to come?" Jack asked.

His mother looked exasperated. "I'm sorry," she said to JJ
before answering the kid. "Jack, you could at least wait for
JJ to leave before you petition me to be excused."

He looked confused for a second but then turned to JJ
and said, "Sorry. It's not you. It's like, dinner and stuff, you
know? And I have like, plans, which my mom kind of knows
about."

"No need to apologize," JJ replied. "If I was fourteen I
wouldn't want to have dinner either." Jack smiled at Susan,
as though he'd just been vindicated, and Susan smiled back,
a brief silent conversation of playful facial expressions passing between them.

Ed spoke then, saying like he'd just remembered it, "Oh, I
have to go down to Washington in the morning, just for a
day or two. Someone's in town and I want to see him before
he goes again."

"Which reminds me," JJ said to Ed before Susan could respond, "I'll go and get that phone number for you, while I
think of it."

"Thanks," said Ed.

"Well this all sounds very intriguing," Susan said, looking
at Ed for an explanation.

"That's why you wouldn't have made a spy, Susan. Don't
see connections when they're not there. See, the phone number JJ has for me is an old friend from Berlin who lives in
Paris nowadays." She asked if it was anyone she knew, and JJ
excused himself as Ed answered.

He went back through into the inn and up to his room, picking up the passports and putting them in his pocket, finding a piece of paper and writing what looked like a Paris number on it. When he got back to the kitchen though, Ed wasn't there. Susan looked up from her paperwork to say, "He's gone up to his room, third door on the left-hand side."

"Thanks," said JJ and walked up to Ed's room, a guest room that looked similar to JJ's a little way beyond the partition.

Standing in the open doorway, he went through the form of giving him the phone number, chatting inanely while handing over the passports. Ed responded likewise, talking about nothing as he flicked through them and put them away. They parted then, saying they'd see each other at dinner, Ed closing his door.

As JJ walked back toward the top of the stairs he noticed one of the other doors he'd passed half open, giving a view of the room from that direction, a narrow glimpse of what looked like the girl's room, a few posters on the wall. He slowed down, staring in as he passed, suddenly noticing the reflection in the mirror above the cluttered dressing table, the girl herself and her boyfriend, asleep on the bed like two entwined children, a spellbound sense of stillness about them.

Seeing them there reminded him of a winter afternoon years before when he'd been about her age, sleeping fully clothed with his girlfriend, waking a little and watching the light fade, feeling her close, one of those rare moments that had been beautiful at the time and not just in the recollection.

He hadn't thought of it in years but did now because of seeing them, the sleeping September-lit room pumping blood back into that part of his memory. And he felt envious too, of their youth, their clean slate, or perhaps just of the

PEOPLE DIE   163

boyfriend, for having someone or something to hold on to, for having her.

Because despite what Ed had said, it still seemed hard to believe that he'd ever find a balance like that again. There had been Aurianne for a while, and for a while that had felt like something stable, but he hadn't even loved her, and the worst part of that was knowing how devastated he'd have been now if they had been in love.

No doubt Ed would have countered that the present situation was a one-time thing, nothing to govern life choices by, but they worked in a business that had a way of throwing up one-time situations like that. If it was just him that wouldn't matter, but he didn't see how he could ever invest in a life beyond himself, not fully invest, not knowing what he knew.

Bostridge perhaps had been lucky. He'd been an amateur, not a real player. So it had been only Bostridge himself who'd been killed. Apart from his death, as much of a loss as that must have been, his family had been immune, to the extent that here they were blindly playing host to two people intimately involved with the killing and yet able to continue with life as normal: boyfriends, discussions about work and school, dinners with the friends of friends.

Following Jack's exit JJ had reckoned on just the three adults having dinner, but when he got there the kitchen table was set for four. There was no food cooking, though. Susan brusquely dismissed her own cooking skills, explaining that the meal would be brought in, double-checking that JJ liked beef.

The three of them were already sitting down when Jem came in, a vague smile on her face, like a contentment spilling over from some other part of her life. She was wearing a summery dress but with a white T-shirt under it, show-

ing up the light tan of her skin, the dress offering brief hints
of the figure beneath as she moved, her breasts, hips, all subtle promise.

JJ started to stand up but thought better of it, not wanting to embarrass her, rising from his seat only to shake hands
when Susan introduced them. Her hand was soft but with a
firmer grip than her brother's, determined, her eyes pale
green, searching again as if trying to read code.

She was sitting opposite him but didn't speak for a while,
listening instead as JJ and the others made small talk. A couple of times their eyes met but averted quickly, the girl looking mildly flustered each time. There was something amusing
about it, and something strangely reassuring too, that there
was already some indistinct chemistry between the two of
them, a girl almost half his age, a teenager whose father he'd
killed when she'd still been a child.

The food came, beef in a rich sauce, mushrooms, beer
perhaps. Ed tasted his and said, "Wonderful. JJ should eat
with us more often." Susan laughed at the backhanded insult
to her cooking, and Jem joined in then, speaking for the first
time since sitting down. "No, Mom, this is like, so good."
The same affected hesitancy as her brother and what seemed
like most other American kids.

"Honestly, JJ," Susan said, "my cooking isn't wonderful
but it really isn't as bad as all that."

"I'm sure it isn't. This is very good though."

Ed cut in, picking up on what Susan had just said. "I like
that chicken thing you make. But really, Susan, there's no
shame in not being a great cook." He turned to JJ then. "She
was raised on the Upper East Side and the Hamptons; till she
was eighteen she thought food came ready-cooked."

Susan and Jem laughed, Jem suddenly saying a little too

hastily afterward, "So like, why do they call you JJ? I mean, when your name's William Hoffman."

He wondered if she'd checked his name in the register, maybe after first seeing him the previous night. "Childhood nickname," he said. "Doesn't mean anything."

"And why are you called Hoffman?" He felt a slight charge, the fact that she was curious about him, bemused at the same time that it mattered to him.

"It's my father's name."

"But it's not English, right?"

"Nor is he. He's Swiss. I live in Switzerland too."

"Oh." She seemed to think about it for a second or two and then added, "Cool." She said no more then for the rest of the meal, just listening again, more relaxed now though whenever their eyes met, even smiling a couple of times in response.

They'd finished eating when her boyfriend appeared behind her in the doorway. Susan introduced him to JJ and the kid said, "Yeah, we met, kind of. Hey."

"Hello, Freddie."

"So, um . . . ," Jem said to her mother questioningly, like she wasn't sure of the polite thing to do.

"Well, Freddie could join us," said Susan, "but as we're not in formal society I think we can probably spare the two of you." The girl smiled, excusing herself, offering a general good-bye to the room as much as to the people in it, Freddie saying bye to each of them, an innate politeness forcing its way out past the surface cool.

Susan waited till they'd gone and said quietly then, "I do worry about them. They're in love, there's no doubt about that, but I have a bad feeling Freddie Sales will break her heart."

She actually seemed fairly relaxed about the prospect, but Ed looked stern and said, "Then he'll be making a big mistake, won't he, JJ?"

"She's a beautiful girl," he agreed. Susan looked flattered, but Ed looked nonplussed, saying, "I don't mean that! I mean he'll be messing with the wrong people."

"Speak for yourself," said Susan quickly, "JJ and I are the right kind of people." Ed acknowledged the wordplay. JJ felt flattered this time, by her tone and by the feeling around the table of complete acceptance, as if they'd known him for years rather than days.

And the fact that they'd been connected for almost two years hardly seemed to matter as they sat there, or what connected them. On the surface it was a freak encounter that the four of them had been brought together at that table, the way storms left strange fish sharing the same rock pools. But at some deeper level it felt right to be there, a place where he seemed to belong.

It was the feeling he got with Jem, too, based on no more than a few glances, on the indefinable attraction he felt toward her, that there was something prewritten between them, some unspoken territories that they already shared. It was ridiculous, a grown man losing sight of things because of the attraction of a pretty girl, but that was how he felt, Berg, Naumenko, and everything else almost fading against the thought of her.

13

There were fewer people at the breakfast table the next morning. Kathryn ran through the guests who'd departed the previous day or who'd eaten early and departed that morning, pointing out that it would be a full house again by the evening.

It was Lenny and Dee's last day too. JJ went through the ritual of tea and coffee in the lounge with them, though without the papers this time, the couple talking instead about the trip home and how they couldn't wait to see the kids again.

He saw them off when they were leaving, Dee hugging him, Lenny giving him a business card with their address and phone number written on the back, an open invitation to visit, all for someone they'd known perhaps four or five hours in total.

Once they'd gone he stood there for a minute, trying to decide whether to walk down to the village but not moving, preferring to enjoy the moment, another blue sky and the faint hollow chill in the air, the winter's promise that was loaded into autumn mornings.

Suddenly Jem walked past wearing jeans, heavy boots, a flannel shirt, her hair hanging down over the back of it, almost flaxen in the early sun. After a few paces she stopped, as if realizing who was standing there. She turned and looked at him, covering her eyes against the sunlight. "Hey, JJ."

"Good morning."

"Are you walking?"

"Just to the village."

"Me too. I mean, if you wanna tag along?"

"Sure," he said and walked with her, saying, "No school today?"

"It's Saturday," she replied, looking at him like she couldn't believe how out of touch he was. It was a shock to him too, that he'd visited Viner that Sunday and then lost himself afterward, time blurring, life blurring, a week falling away from him.

"So shouldn't you be, oh, I don't know, at the mall or something?"

"I hate malls. Honestly," she said, glancing at him. "I'm like, so untypical of your average American teenager. I mean, what is this teenager thing anyway, right? It's just like some kind of marketing thing."

"I think the whole of life is a marketing thing."

"I guess you're right." She pointed at a knotted old tree and said, "We used to have a tree house up there. One winter when I was like, ten or something, it just fell apart."

"I had a tree house when I was a kid."

"What happened to it?"

"It's still there," he said, thinking of it now, thinking how it didn't even seem that long ago. There were still remnants visible in the tree Jem had pointed at too, hidden to strangers but there all the same, just as the whole of the surrounding area was probably filled with the markers of her childhood, places that were significant to her alone.

"So what's it like," she asked, "where you live?"

"Where I live now? Geneva. It's a city but it's okay. It's on a lake." For the first time since flying to London he thought about going back there, what it would mean, whether he still wanted to be there. He was pretty certain now that one way or another he'd have that option of return, that sooner or later it would be safe again, but the city itself suddenly seemed alien in his memory. "I'm thinking about moving sometime soon," he added, the thought spilling out as it occurred to him, "maybe to the mountains."

"Do you have a girlfriend?"

"No. I just broke up with someone, after two years."

"Oh. That sucks."

"Yeah," said JJ, knowing that breaking up wouldn't have sucked, that what sucked was Aurianne being beaten, abused, bruised with the cold metal of the barrel, a bullet thumping her down into the carpet; that was what sucked.

Suddenly he heard Jem say, "Are you okay?"

He laughed, responding, "Sorry, I'm fine, I was just thinking about something." She smiled back at him, a smile that looked tinged with admiration somehow, a look he didn't quite understand.

"I know how you feel," she said. "I guess I'd feel the same way if me and Freddie broke up, which we will I guess but, you know, it's like we've been together for, well, kind of forever really." He returned her smile, amused more than anything by the stumbling delivery, by the perception of time. Yet as she talked on about Freddie he felt his earlier envy returning, a sense that for all the hassles of being a teenager, and despite the loss of her father, she was still living through halcyon days. He had a sense that she knew it too, a level of self-knowledge that constantly evaded him in his own life, a life that was lived blind, forever stumbling from one piece of furniture to the next.

They passed the first few houses, a woman waving at Jem from an upstairs window, Jem waving back like she hadn't seen her in months. There was more traffic on the roads, more people too than there had been during the week, an occupying army that probably left the locals ambivalent about how picturesque their town was.

Jem stopped when they got to the church, set back from the road but with a handful of tourists wandering around on the lawn, staring, photographing it like it was an architectural wonder.

"Where were you heading?" she asked JJ then.

"Nowhere in particular."

"Oh, right, only, this is where I'm going."

"To church?"

"No," she said, laughing. "My dad's grave. I mean, if you wanna come, it's okay and everything." JJ felt his system grind up a gear as he got it, a sudden hammer-blow awareness of the obvious, that Bostridge was buried there, that there had been a funeral, that they visited his grave.

Surprisingly until now, even being among them, the link between him and the Bostridges had hardly seemed to matter, like it was nothing more than a metaphysical exercise to pass the time, no basis in reality. And in the family too it had seemed like no one was missing, that there were no gaps, but there was a gap and here he was facing it. "Perhaps I won't," he said, stumbling a little over the words. "I'm sure you'd rather be alone."

"Okay," she replied breezily, seeing his discomfort maybe. She laughed then and said, "It's okay, you know. I won't be like, overcome with emotion or anything. I just like to visit." He could see that she wanted him to go with her, and felt embarrassed that he'd come across as so retentive, like he couldn't have dealt with the possibility of her being upset at her father's grave.

They walked along the side of the church, passing a few graves; most of them were to the rear though with trees among them, the leaves catching the breeze. As at the front there were tourists, studying the headstones, their voices occasionally audible against the papery rustling that rose and fell on a wind too slight to be felt.

Bostridge's headstone was simple, understated, the barest facts and the simple quote "So we'll go no more a-roving." JJ recognized it, a poem by Byron, and wondered if it spoke of a man he couldn't have imagined from their brief programmed encounter, a romantic, someone in whose imagination the world had been colored by his dreaming. That sounded more like the person Holden had described too, a person who, had he been removed from the visceral truth of it, might even have found his own death romantic. Perhaps if JJ hadn't been there he'd have been able to see it that way too.

There were flowers in front of the headstone but Jem didn't touch them or the stone itself, just stood at the foot of the grave, praying perhaps or speaking her thoughts to him or simply lost in thought, her face serenely composed, like time had suspended itself around her. JJ stood to the side and back a pace, conscious of intruding.

He studied her as she stood there, struck again by the way she looked, the way she was, the kind of prettiness that was hard to reduce to specifics. She was still a kid, beyond reach in his own way of things, but he was drawn to her all the same, drawn at a level hidden beyond reasoning, neurons firing along unfamiliar pathways. And maybe the way she looked was only part of it anyway, because there were plenty of young girls who were as beautiful, a shallow swell of beauty that was everywhere with girls of that age.

Briefly he wondered if the attraction was in the connection with Bostridge himself or even with the girl in Moscow, a girl who'd drawn him just as much, tapping into his psyche, burying an image of herself there, a girl he'd thought of too when he'd first seen Jem. It was a simpler attraction than that though, the kind of subconscious recognition of compatibility that happened all the time in ordinary lives, the fact that she was David Bostridge's daughter merely a cruel trick of fate.

She turned and smiled, signifying that she was finished, and as they walked away said, "Would you like to go for a coffee or something?"

"Or something would be nice; I don't drink coffee."

"Me either," she said, like it was a massive coincidence.

"Oh, and as long as it isn't the Cheese Press or the Old Maple Tavern."

"No, there is another place." She laughed then and added as if to herself, "This town is *so* weird!" They went to a small café that also sold local crafts, pottery, carved ornaments; people browsed around them, looking at the goods on display as they talked and drank lemon tea.

They talked for a long while, background filling, getting to know each other. It was something he was used to, used to lying his way through, a lie that was like his own life but off-kilter, an information drift that left his real existence in the shadows. Even Aurianne had known only a rehearsed version of himself.

But as easily as all of that came to him, it wasn't what he did with Jem; the real JJ spilled out instead, devoid only of the death and the killing that usually dominated his life but here seemed to leave no readily apparent blank spaces, Jem satisfied that she was talking to a full, rounded person.

It was only in the innocuous detail of his life that he was being open with her, but those had been the details he'd been most cagey about in the past, like they were the key to cracking him open and getting the rest. And he didn't know why he was choosing to be open with her like that, perhaps because of having met Jools again or because of the easiness he'd found in Holden and the rest of them, perhaps only because the last week had taught him that being cagey didn't deliver very much.

Whatever the reasons, it was liberating to sit there with her and share stories of their childhoods and families, and of love, relationships, of the common ground they had between them. It was liberating for once to meet someone new and feel only an unhindered desire to share personal histories, with no caution, no uneasiness, and, maybe most ironic of all, with no baggage.

He liked being with her, liked the way she spoke, the way her eyes came alive when she was talking about something, the way she broke into an easy smile, becoming bashful then when he asked what she was smiling about. He liked simply sitting opposite her, being able to look into her face.

It was just one of those rare encounters, a language quickly emerging between them, and it was something again

that reminded him of being her age, of the growing teenage
awareness that there were other people out there to connect
with, the feeling of no longer being isolated.

They walked back to the inn together afterward, a sense
of having come to know each other well in the hours since
they'd walked out together, and as they passed the church
she said, "I'm glad you came to my dad's grave with me."

It was a strange thing to say, even now, and he let a note of
confusion creep into his voice as he asked, "Why?"

"I don't know," she said, "it's just like, kind of cool that
you came."

"You must miss him," JJ said, thinking maybe she'd
shared the same closeness with her father that Jack had with
Susan.

"Not really," she said, answering casually, backing herself
up then. "It was Thanksgiving when it happened." That was
right; it had been a Thursday, Thanksgiving, and Bostridge
had chosen to spend it there, inadvertently choosing the day
of his execution, inadvertently tainting every future Thanksgiving for his family too.

"So?" asked JJ, questioning the statement as a matter of
form.

"So it wasn't like, unusual for him to be away for Thanksgiving and stuff. I guess what I'm saying is, it's hard to miss
someone who wasn't there that much."

"I suppose you're right. A lot of people are in the same
position though. You know, business."

She looked at him earnestly, as if he needed to be reassured. "Oh, I don't like, blame him or anything. And I
guess I miss what we might have had together but . . ." She
trailed off, adding then, "Let's not talk about my dad. I'm
glad you came to his grave, that's all." She seemed bored by

the subject rather than uncomfortable with it; she'd probably spoken about it a lot in the time since, everyone wanting to talk about it with her, demanding catharsis the way
people did.

So they chatted about other things for the rest of the way,
talking less though. And when they got back to the inn they
stood in the lobby and said bye to each other, dwelling a little
over it, stilted pauses before she said finally, "Am I keeping
you? I mean, do you have plans or anything?"

"No, not at all," he said quickly, the signal clear. She
smiled again in response, an edge in her eyes he couldn't
quite read.

"Good," she said then. "There's something I wanna show
you." She led him into their side of the house, a stillness in
there, of stopped clocks, nobody else home. As he followed
her up the stairs he realized they were going to her room, the
one where he'd seen her lost in sleep with Freddie; a low-level
buzz of anticipation caught him at the thought of it.

It meant nothing to her though to be taking him there.
She casually cleared some discarded clothes from the bed as
she led him in, saying, "Take a seat," as she threw them into
a closet. There was a small armchair in one corner, a chair
too in front of the desk where she had books open, half-
finished homework, but he sat on one side of the large bed
and took in the teenage clutter, the way the whole of her life
was jumbled into that space.

His room at home was still similar in that respect, very
much the room of the younger JJ but without the presence
that had made it, like he'd died in his late teens and his parents had kept it as a shrine. His sister's room was different,
altered in some way or other every time she was home, a
room that was still alive, the one too into which guests were

put when space was running short, his nearly always left empty, frozen, waiting for him to return.

Jem was rummaging in the bottom of the closet, opening different boxes, standing up then with a large shoe box in her hands. She walked over and sat cross-legged farther up the bed from him, putting the box down between them.

He hadn't noticed her taking her boots off, but they'd gone, the sight of her feet in blue woolen socks suddenly giving him a feeling of enticing intimacy, a subtle marker to show that things had changed imperceptibly. He'd been with her all morning, but he was in her personal space now, the place where she felt most at ease, sitting together on the bed where she slept, close enough that he could almost feel her presence, his mind subconsciously registering her scent.

She opened the box and then smiled at him before saying, "This is what I wanna show you." She handed him a photograph, kept smiling as he looked down at it, like she couldn't wait to see his response.

It was a photograph of two young guys, students, facing the camera with big full-of-life smiles, the pair of them lean and all clean-cut exuberance. The slightly taller of the two had his arm over the other's shoulder but was pulling it in against his neck as if about to choke him, the smaller guy's smile even bigger because of the horseplay. It was a good picture, poignant somehow, a moment of pure laughter captured intact.

It looked like it had been taken in the late sixties maybe, the time frame suggesting itself because the smaller guy was David Bostridge, an uncanny prediction of how Jack would look in just a few years.

JJ looked up and said, "Your dad?"

"No," she said, like he didn't get it, then qualified her reply, "I mean, yeah, but it's not just Dad. It's Dad and Ed, when they were at Dartmouth." He looked at the picture again, seeing the resemblance now in the bone structure, despite the dark hair, the fresh face.

And more now as he looked at it he could see the closeness between the two of them, a bond apparent even in that snapped moment. It brought home to him, too, the magnitude of the place Holden had finally come to with that friend, the ceremonial sanctioning of his death.

Holden probably found it hard even to look at pictures like that now, the whole sweep of their friendship caught up in those youthful smiles, the knowledge of how it ended seeming hidden somehow in the grain of the photo, in the blurred sunlight. Even as it was, and for all his professionalism, there must undoubtedly have been times when Holden castigated himself for having done so little on Bostridge's behalf, that he hadn't tried to tip him off, that he hadn't questioned Berg's operation.

Jem began to talk as JJ looked at the picture. "I think my dad was happier there than any other time in his whole life. I mean, he was such a hero and everything, I'm sure nothing else ever lived up to it." She was right; he had the look on his face of someone who knew it was his time, popularity worn lightly, a life lived easily. Maybe it was the feeling he'd been trying to recapture in Russia, a reminder for himself of who he'd once been.

"There are different kinds of happiness," JJ said, looking up. "I know what you mean though." He glanced briefly back at the picture and added, "What about Ed? He looks pretty happy too."

"Ed's different. I think he's had more, you know, balance. I'd guess he's as happy now as when that picture was taken. Well, except for the business over Dad and everything, but then, those things happen, don't they? It's just life." JJ nodded, not saying anything, and Jem took another picture out of the box, swapping it for the one of Holden and Bostridge. "My mom when she was my age." He looked at it, a posed picture, a portrait maybe or a yearbook photo. Her hair was longer but she didn't look like Jem, as he'd expected, and looked only vaguely like herself as she was now, a pretty girl but with none of the woman's poise.

"Oh," he said, registering his surprise. "I thought the two of you looked alike but Susan doesn't look like you at all here."

"She's prettier," Jem offered, her tone completely serious.

"Different, not prettier." She smiled as if dismissing his flattery, a glimpse again of her age, the fact that, in spite of the obvious evidence, in spite of people telling her constantly, she still didn't have the measure of her own beauty.

He smiled too and said, "You don't dare believe it, and maybe that's a good thing too, but you *are* beautiful." Her smile almost broke into a laugh but she blushed slightly too. "And now I've embarrassed you. I'm sorry."

"No, you haven't," she said, reassuring him. She hesitated then, her mouth poised like she wanted to say something else, the thought unformed though, as if she couldn't put the words together in the right order. He thought of saying something but waited silently instead, eager to know where she was heading, and then the phone rang next to her bed. Jem ignored it at first, looking visibly frustrated as she finally leaned over and picked it up.

"Hello?" Her tone shifted as she added, "Hey." Whatever she'd been thinking about those few seconds before had slipped back into the depths, JJ left tantalized by the thought of where the conversation might have gone. Perhaps it was best that it was lost though, and that she was smiling now to the sound of the voice at the other end of the phone, a voice he guessed was Freddie's.

He put the photo back on top of the other in the box and stood; Jem looked troubled in response. "Hold on," she said into the phone and looked up at him. "You don't have to leave. I mean, I don't mind if you stay." She looked frustrated again that the phone call had interrupted them.

He smiled apologetically and said, "No, I should make a move. Thanks though. I've enjoyed today."

"Me too." He made his way out, Jem continuing into the phone, "Oh, JJ, you know. I was like, showing him old photos and stuff." It seemed strange that it had meant only that to her, looking at old photos, a sentiment on her part that was painful to think about, because it meant that all of what he thought had developed between them in the previous hours was corrupted, all the sense of connection, of belonging, of finding someone important.

He doubted anyway that his company had meant as much to her as hers had to him. Because he was left wired by it, a feeling he'd left behind long ago, back in those old photos he'd looked at with Jools, maybe even before. It was as if being with her had reminded him temporarily of who he'd once been, reminded, not as he had been with Jools, by memories, but by finding it still within him.

For a while there, sitting with Jem on her bed, already familiar, it had been like the previous ten years had never happened. That was the remarkable thing about her, that in her company his own history seemed erased, of no importance, and yet it was a history in which she herself was inextricably linked, part of the fabric in a way she'd never know.

14

Susan knocked on his door a little later. JJ offered her a seat but Susan preferred to stand, saying she wouldn't keep him. There was a slight awkwardness like JJ was already falling somewhere between being a guest and being a friend.

The feeling was reinforced as she said, "I don't want to press you and, really, you might be tired of us already, I'd quite understand. Only, I've invited a few friends over for dinner this evening, partly, well, mainly because Ed was here. And now he's torn off down to Washington. But if you'd like to come, you'd be more than welcome. I mean, if you don't mind making up the numbers?"

"Not at all, and on the contrary, I'm surprised you're not tired of me. I feel like a gate-crasher."

She smiled as if he'd suggested something ridiculous. "Good," she said, mentally checking it off. "By the way, Jem mentioned that you'd walked with her this morning, to David's grave and everything. I just wanted to . . . well, to thank you I suppose. I mean, sometimes I worry; I don't think she connects with many people, so it's nice when she does. It's nice that you made the effort."

"It was no effort," said JJ, smiling then, "and maybe it's good that she's choosy about who she mixes with."

Susan smiled too, slightly scornful, and said, "That's exactly what Ed says. You people, you all think alike, all paranoid." Not as paranoid as some, he thought, not as paranoid as Berg for example. But then for the moment, with Holden in Washington sorting things out, Berg seemed to matter less than ever.

Dinner passed the evening. Susan's friends were curious about him, about Switzerland, one couple eager to know how Tom Furst was doing in London. Susan looked pleased to have him there too, falling just short of showing him off in front of them.

He was disappointed, though, that the kids weren't there, a vague feeling that what they were doing was probably more interesting, riper with opportunity, out there in the experimental shallows of life. And, in truth, it was just Jem that he missed, an almost teenage petulance on his part that she preferred to be elsewhere, that perhaps the friendship they'd struck up that day counted even less for her than he'd thought.

It made sense that it should be like that anyway. Because as much common ground as there had seemed between them, he wasn't a teenager and she was still unformed, browsing through life. It was strange, though, that he felt more of an impostor among Susan's friends than he had sitting on Jem's bed with her, looking at photos of her parents, talking like equals.

Jack put his head around the door later to say he was back

and was called in then to face a barrage of compliments; he
backed off again as quickly as possible. Soon after, JJ made
his own excuses and left, realizing Holden would most likely
be back the next day, wanting to have had a good night's
sleep in case it was bad news. Even good news would mean
that he could move on, just as he was almost taking to being
there, finding reasons to stay, getting used to the routine.

He was even becoming a part of the routine. Kathryn introduced some of the new guests at breakfast the next morning like he was an old-timer. JJ took his tea and papers alone
in the lounge afterward, missing the presence of Lenny and
Dee with their inane dissection of the world's news. Even the
sky was overcast as if in response to their absence.

He'd been there only twenty minutes though when Jem
came in. "Hey," she said, and then, "mind if I join you?"

"Of course not. Would you like tea? I can get another
cup."

"No, don't, I'll go." She walked through to the dining
room and came back a moment later with a cup and saucer,
saying as she poured her tea, "Jack and Mom have gone to
church. I wasn't up in time."

"Do you go every week?"

"No, but I like to go." She thought about it for a second
and added, "I like that I can just, kind of, think of nothing,
you know? I like that." JJ nodded his understanding and
then, changing the subject she said, "How long are you staying here?"

"I don't know," he said, the various possibilities of what
would happen next already played out in his mind. "Tomorrow, maybe the day after."

She looked disappointed, in her eyes, her mouth, in every
muscle of her face, a faintly visible contraction of disap-
pointment. "Will you come back?" she asked.

"I think so." She smiled in response, open and unguarded, eliciting a smile from him too. "You know, when I arrived the other day, I wasn't at all sure about this place, the other guests, the village. But it's grown on me, and it's hard to believe how comfortable I've felt with all of you. And all because I know Tom."

"That wouldn't have counted for much if we hadn't liked you." He acknowledged the point and she asked, "So like, when do you think you'll be back?" He'd said yes to his earlier question, but now she was asking for specifics, forcing him to consider how likely it was that he really would come back. It seemed doubtful somehow but he wanted to imagine some future return, wanted to imagine seeing her. He didn't want to disappoint her either, have her think that she'd opened up the previous day to someone who really was a stranger, someone she'd never see again. So he said, "Every time I'm in New York," inventing an imaginary work schedule that brought him over regularly, saying then, "possibly the end of next month. I tend to be here every couple of months anyway."

She nodded, but her concentration seemed to get caught by something else, like there was a producer screaming instructions into her earpiece, and then without warning she asked, as if it had been troubling her, "Were you in love with her? The girl you broke up with?" She responded quickly to his expression, adding, "I'm sorry, that's really rude of me."

He smiled, brushing it off as he said, "No, it was the sudden change of subject that threw me, not the question."

"Oh," she said and laughed then, realizing what she'd done. He laughed too, intrigued though that it had been on her mind, and a few seconds later he said, "To answer your question, no, I wasn't. We liked each other a lot, but we weren't in love."

"Have you ever? I don't think you said."

"Been in love?" She nodded. "Oh yeah, a long time ago though." He thought about it but could see in her face that she wanted more, adding with an indulgent smile, "Let me see, her name was Emily, we were at college, it was good while it lasted. What more can I say?"

"What happened? I mean, why did it end?"

"I don't know," he said, shaking his head. "I suppose we changed. See, I liked to think she finished it, because I was still in love with her even after it was over. But apparently she was still in love with me too. Yet it got to a stage where we could barely sit in the same room together. I don't know, it was just messy, and we were young. She's married now, they're both teachers. They have two children."

Jem sat in silence for a moment, looking almost saddened, adding then in a distracted aside, "Do you still think about her?" For a couple of years he had, all the time, but not now; he wasn't sure he even remembered what it was to think about someone like that.

"Occasionally," he said, "in passing, but I stopped being in love with her a long time ago too, and there's been no one else since."

"You'll fall in love again though," she said, pitched halfway between question and statement, like she needed re-assurance.

"Of course," said JJ, casually, giving it little enough thought to believe in it himself for the moment, "I'm sure I will." That seemed to satisfy her, whatever track it was she'd been following, and she changed the subject again, talking about the movie she'd seen with Freddie the previous night, going back to his house, a quick biography of the Sales family, subjects meshing into each other, questions to JJ as they occurred to her, the conversation open-ended like one they'd continue in the times ahead of them.

A couple of times as they talked he thought back to those questions about love, questions that had come across as crucially important to her, as though she had some deep concern for his emotional welfare. And it took him a while to realize that the questions hadn't been about him at all but had been a sounding board for whatever was going on in her own life, between her and Freddie or whoever else.

Yet she'd have been right to be concerned about him, because all of his emotions had been smothered, mechanized, things he expressed through memory rather than reflex. And maybe that was why he was drawn to people like the girl in Moscow, Jem herself, because they were beyond reach, and it was easier for him to keep feelings like that at a distance.

The remainder of the tea had long gone cold in their cups when Jem's eyes skipped to the door and she said, "Hey, Ed." She jumped up and kissed him on the cheek, telling him to sit down with JJ while she got some coffee. JJ asked him about his journey, biding his time till she came back. She asked the same questions then before leaving without ceremony, taking the tea things with her.

Once they were alone Ed let a lazy satisfied smile creep across his face and said, "Korzhakov and Mavrodi were Naumenko's men; we're in business."

JJ's head cleared, coming around quickly to the real business of his being there, to what he did, the half of him that Jem hadn't unearthed. "So what's next?" he asked.

"Naumenko's in Athens. I've taken the liberty of getting you a ticket for tomorrow."

"Me? Why not you?" A voice started in his head, a voice which had first sounded in the bookstore with Tom, and if it was a setup this would be the perfect sting. His gut though was telling him that Holden was okay, and that no one, not even Berg, would engineer a setup that elaborate anyway. He still didn't like the idea of a face-to-face with Naumenko, but he knew that was how those people worked and Ed was already explaining why it had to be him.

"I don't know if Naumenko would believe me. Like I said, he never forgave me for David so he might not trust my intentions here. You on the other hand"—Ed nodded like he was impressed by his own reasoning—"you'll have him eating out of your hand. I know the man, and I know your reputation, and he'll admire you even more for having the balls to just walk in there."

"Who says I have the balls?" JJ said, smiling, adding a second later, "Okay I'll go, but I'll book my own ticket."

Ed raised his eyebrows and said, "You can trust me, you know, JJ." He looked hurt that JJ was suspicious, even now, but it was a sentiment that probably didn't go much beneath the surface.

"I know I can; it's just a superstition of mine." It was partly trust, even with Holden, but it was partly superstition too, a feeling that it would be bad luck to take an air ticket from someone else. And thinking of it now brought back a memory of Aurianne again, telling him how safe air travel was, how much more likely it was to be killed some other way, any other way.

Even so, he'd buy his own ticket, and this time in remembering Aurianne he thought of Jem too, the brief flowering of friendship he'd found here with her in these couple of days, a simple reawakening of what it meant to be with a person and feel wired because of it.

It was enough to make him want to come back here as

he'd said he would, to follow some of Holden's advice and find part of his future with them, people whose past he'd also partly written. He doubted it would happen like that though, suspected that in the end he'd find himself unable to take that path, opting for the obvious one instead.

He'd go to Athens, sort things out with Naumenko, get his life back into operational mode. And for all his week of introspection he'd probably just slip back into the shadows like he normally did, taking the easiest route, just as he had two years before, leaving the girl behind in the sleet darkness, avoiding the truths she might have had to impart, returning to what he already knew.

Suddenly Ed cut in on his train of thought, tentatively, as if waking him. "JJ, you don't have to do this if you don't want to." He looked like he meant it too; perhaps the wound of Bostridge's death was showing itself again, the fear that he might be sending someone else to his death.

"I know I don't," JJ said casually, "but it's what I do. It means no more to me than"—he tried to think of something and said finally—"than boarding a plane."

"But you'll still buy your own ticket," Ed said, smiling, JJ smiling too in acknowledgment.

"I'll still buy my own ticket." That was it, as if deciding when to fly determined everything else that followed, as if the difference between life and death was all a matter of choosing the right airline, the right flight, the right destination. It was how people kept going, by believing it was all that simple.

15

How close had they come those two years before? What additional factor would it have taken for the pilot to have lost control, for the plane to have come flailing out of its climb, tearing itself into scrap, burned bodies flung over the frozen hinterland of the airport?

The plane had never been in danger, that's what Aurianne had said and always stuck to. He thought about it though. Every time he flew he turned it over again, not out of fear, more out of curiosity, the curiosity of a bystander with no great stake in whether he lived or died.

It was out of his hands, that's what appealed to him. This plane that he was sitting on now, waiting to take off in a calm night sky, could explode like others had before it, scattering him and everyone else into the ocean, reducing their lives to debris to be picked from the water with seats and suitcases.

It was almost a comforting thought, the prospect of his

reputation and his history and all the unwritten killings ahead of him, dispersed in the inky water of the Atlantic, leaving behind only the body of a venture capitalist, somebody with two parents, a sister, no other connections.

"Oh God!"

JJ turned to look at the woman next to him, gray haired, early sixties, somebody's grandmother. He'd been conscious of her, tense and uneasy, and now the plane was taxiing and she'd felt the need to let someone else know how nervous she was. She smiled apologetically but JJ put his hand on hers where it clenched the armrest and fixed her gaze. "This plane won't crash," he said, quiet, forceful.

"I know, it's silly of me."

"No it isn't. Planes do crash and any rational person has every right to be afraid. But this plane won't; it's not how you die, it's not how I die. Trust me." She looked transfixed for a moment or two, mystified, enchanted, the placebo effect of his words taking hold of her like a prophetic truth. She nodded then and leaned back with her eyes closed, her hand relaxing beneath his.

JJ relaxed too as the plane began to pull underneath him. He'd meant well but was left bemused by how easy it was to make someone believe she'd live forever. And maybe it was a spell he'd cast on himself too, a belief that he'd never take a bullet, a stubborn underlying resistance even now to the reality of what he was flying into, a reality he knew better than he pretended.

Twenty minutes or so into the flight the woman opened her eyes again and said, "Thank you so much."

"It was nothing," replied JJ, turning to her.

"Oh it was though." She stared at him again. "I could see in your eyes that you know about these things."

"More than I care to," he said, smiling. They talked on and off then throughout the flight, between the movie and sleeping, JJ finding himself surprisingly expansive about Vermont and the Copley. And when they arrived in the harsh haze-filled sunlight of Athens she thanked him again, like he was the only reason she was still alive. It made him feel good, to know that if it all went wrong he'd done at least one worthwhile thing in the final days.

It was late afternoon by the time he arrived at the hotel, a place he'd never stayed before, as obvious as it was on the city landscape. He showered, ate in his room, ventured in the evening down to the bar, a place with plenty of red leather chairs in classic styles, like some garish seventies attempt at an English club.

If he'd been playing by the rules he'd have stayed away from the public areas but he liked the idea of being out in the open, the possibility that someone would identify him or that, best of all, Berg himself would stroll nonchalantly into the bar and see JJ sitting there.

Berg wasn't that nonchalant though, perhaps not even nonchalant enough to be in the same hotel as the man who was protecting him, and the Russians themselves were probably too tightly leashed to be down there relaxing. Instead, JJ took his couple of drinks alone at the bar, a few people talking quietly in other parts of the room, the barman keeping to himself. And after the two drinks he made it an early night, already tired, feeling he'd held off long enough to beat the jet lag.

He slept fitfully though, angry sleep, waking more than once with a pounding reflex, springing out of the bed before coming to and realizing there was no threat. The second time woke him fully, enough for him to put the lamp on and sit there on the edge of the bed, collecting his thoughts. It was just after three, too early to stay awake, particularly with the day he had ahead of him, but his thoughts were like razors, cutting clean. He took a drink from the minibar and went out onto the balcony where the air was cooler or at least had a kind of coolness that was more authentic, an ebb and flow on a faint breeze.

The pool and gardens below were floodlit but empty, most of the hotel in darkness too, even the city beyond subdued. It was early evening back in Vermont and he thought about it for a while as he stood there, mentally slapping himself then and turning his thoughts instead to the Russians two floors above him.

That was what he had to concentrate on, those Russians, dealing with Naumenko. That was why he needed sleep. Because he'd already let things slip enough that week without going in there tired, his mind on other things. If he ended up taking a bullet, he wanted it to be because it was his day to die, not because he'd lost sight of the ball. For as much as he knew though, perhaps they were one and the same thing.

The next morning he sat on a lounge chair in the shade of some drooping palms, the noise of kids from the small pool off to his right, traffic punctuated by beeping horns from beyond the grounds of the hotel. The heat was still fresh, the day still subdued at the edges.

He guessed most people were in conferences and meetings or out sightseeing before the afternoon temperatures cut off the air supply. The main pool was almost empty, just a couple of people plowing up and down. Most of the lounge chairs were vacant too, though a handful were occupied by other people like him, keeping their own company.

It was just over a week since he'd almost come to Athens

from Geneva, and if he'd taken Danny's advice this was the
kind of place he might well have spent that week, thinking
things were blowing over when in reality he'd have been dying by default as he'd lain there in the sun. It was a piece of
advice he'd pass on himself someday: never take a holiday
during a crisis.

He checked his watch and counted his way up the side of
the building to the sixth floor, reckoning he'd head up there
within the next hour. Naumenko was probably up by now
and ready to face the world. JJ felt ready to face him too, the
couple of hours soaking up the early sun restoring him after
the troubled night, any doubts sinking away into the depths.

He was thinking clearly now, coldly aware of the possible
outcomes of going there, the best of which was Naumenko
backing off, or even dealing with Berg himself. If it fell like
that it would be easy enough then for JJ to normalize things,
putting himself back above the politics, particularly now
with Holden onboard.

If it went the other way it would just be the death sentence
he'd been under all week anyway. And then maybe his only
chance would be if Naumenko didn't want him killed there
in the hotel. Either way, as he'd said to Holden, it was probably worth no more thought than the risk of a plane crashing,
or of getting cancer, dying a silent death in old age, any of
the other options.

He went back up to his room, took a shower, put his suit
on, and went back out to the elevator, pressing for the sixth
floor. When the doors opened it looked like he'd stumbled on
a wedding or funeral party, a handful of guys in suits standing around looking nervous in the lobby. They looked at him
with a mix of edginess and suspicion, bristling as he stepped
out of the elevator toward them.

He singled out the one who was closest to him, a small thin guy with slicked-back hair, a glass-eye stare.

"Tell Mr. Naumenko that William Hoffman is here to see him." The guy kept staring at him, raising an eyebrow as if to ask who he was to be giving orders. He turned all the same, a forced nonchalance, like a kid trying to back down without losing face, and as he walked away he told one of the others to search JJ.

JJ slowly opened his jacket, let the guy frisk him, acknowledging the nod when nothing was found. They all stood for a minute and then the first good sign came when the other guy returned looking embarrassed, apologizing to JJ for any disrespect he'd shown him. JJ shrugged it off, mystified all the same as he often was by his own reputation, by the thought of what must have been said in those brief moments as he'd waited by the elevator.

The guy led him along a corridor and into a room which was either part of a suite or had been refurbished specifically for Naumenko to use as an office. There was a large desk over by the window, a couple of sofas, no flowers or ornaments, the only decoration a few more suited men around the edge of the room.

Naumenko was standing in the middle waiting for him, wearing a suit but no tie. It was the first time JJ had seen him, bar the file picture Holden had shown him. The guy was unlike any of the big Mafia bosses he'd seen, in his early thirties, in good shape, hair neatly combed, almost conservative looking, the boss of a computer company perhaps.

When he spoke, though, electricity came off him, crackling around the room, the flunkies tightening a little in readiness at the deep roll of his voice.

"It's a great pleasure, Mr. Hoffman. I take it I may call

you JJ?" The Russian lilt was still there but his English accent was pretty good too; he had the air of someone who relished speaking the language, finding pleasure in the words, the sounds.

"Of course," said JJ. An expensive-looking smile came back at him.

"Excellent. And of course you must call me Alex, none of this formality or patronymics. Please, come and sit down." JJ followed him over to the sofas and sat down opposite him. Naumenko ordered mint tea for them both, saying, "So, I understand you've had a particularly busy week, killing people in London, Geneva, Paris."

"Connecticut, Vermont," said JJ, adding to the list, Naumenko's face showing that he hadn't known about his two men over there. He seemed to brush it off though, and said with a smile, "I studied at Yale, you know?"

"So I heard—it's a small world." He thought about it for a second and added, "I didn't know they were your people, but I would have killed them anyway. See, I know you have unresolved issues with Holden, but he's one of the good guys."

"That's all very well, JJ, but you know perhaps I'm one of the bad guys."

JJ smiled but thought of Tom talking in the bookstore and said, "No, the good guys are the ones still alive at the end of the story."

"Then that's settled." Naumenko laughed, encompassing everyone in the room with his outstretched arms. "We're all good guys." A couple of his people smiled or laughed too, looking uncertain what the joke was but amused all the same.

Naumenko looked at JJ then and said, "So anyway, you're not here to kill me at least. What then did you have in mind?"

"I came here to tell you that I killed David Bostridge."

For the first time in the meeting Naumenko looked as dangerous as his reputation; there was an almost imperceptible shift in his expression but it was clear all the same, a calculated and underplayed fierceness in his eyes, like a button had been pressed, a countdown started. As it stood at that moment, JJ was dead, exactly the reaction he'd expected, hoping only that the second part of his plan would achieve the expected reversal.

Holden had advised against even mentioning it, too aware himself of how deeply Naumenko had felt about his friend, but the way JJ saw it there'd been no other option; it was a piece of information which might be lethal in the open but could be used by Berg to discredit them if he'd kept it concealed. He was glad he'd mentioned it anyway, felt a strange exhilaration coming off the visual death sentence of Naumenko's eyes, as if dealing with it was a challenge that was worthy of him.

The mint tea was brought in, and Naumenko returned to a level of token charm, the clock counting quietly beneath the surface, the end result not in question.

"You know how I felt about David," he said finally. JJ nodded, Naumenko instructing him, "Then explain."

JJ sipped at his tea, found it too hot, and began casually, "The hit came to me through Viner, and until this week I assumed it had come through the normal channels."

"Ours is not to reason why," added Naumenko. It was unclear from his tone whether he was being sarcastic or not.

JJ responded like he was being straight, saying, "Exactly. But it was someone else's hit. They made it look official but it was personal business. This person, though, ran it past Holden."

"Holden knew?" Naumenko said, shocked, maybe angered by it, that Ed hadn't passed the information on.

"Holden knew," confirmed JJ, eager not to make it sound like criticism. "But like I said, he thought David had stood on London's toes, that it was a done deal. So he felt terrible about it, knowing he couldn't do anything to save his friend. What he could do, though, was request someone who'd do it as quickly and cleanly as possible, so he requested me."

Naumenko nodded thoughtfully, taking in perhaps what this information said about Holden, recasting him in the light of it.

"I didn't know any of this, and Bostridge meant nothing to me, but of course I did it quickly and cleanly anyway."

"He was a wonderful man," said Naumenko as if to himself, saddened by the thought of it, even though he was probably more steeped in death than JJ or any of them. "You know, I take nothing on trust, no one. Trust no one. But David . . . he was one of those rare individuals, a man . . ." He thought about it a moment before continuing, "I would have entrusted my life to him. And who else could I say that about? My mother, my wife? Not many more, not even my own brother. So you see, David Bostridge was a special person." His voice was building slowly, becoming more forceful. "And yes, special people are killed in Russia every day, but this was wrong, this was . . ." He ground to a halt, his face tightening, like he could feel the anger surfacing and wanted to hold it back.

The situation was looking more dangerous by the second—Holden's analysis was probably right after all—but JJ couldn't focus on it, drawn instead to the empty expanses that existed in his picture of Bostridge, a man seemingly lightly missed by his own family yet mourned bitterly by someone like Naumenko. There had to have been more to him; the only clue perhaps lay in the photo Jem had shown him, the young confident guy laughing at the camera and everything else ahead of him.

"I didn't know him," JJ said.

Naumenko fixed him with a stare in response, as if trying to interpret what he'd said. "You didn't know him. Yet you think you can come here, throw his death in my face, and walk away again."

JJ nodded, acknowledging the point, and inexplicably it made him think of Jem again, the way she'd looked standing at her father's grave, and then a flood of other memories from that week, a week which had somehow managed to re-animate him, a moment of acute consciousness perhaps, before the inevitable. And if Naumenko was decided on having him killed, then perhaps it was as good a week as any to go out on.

"I don't know, Alex," said JJ, thinking aloud. "Maybe it's my time to die."

The comment seemed to throw Naumenko who looked puzzled and said, "What do you mean?"

What did he mean? He meant it was easier to switch off and step aside, it was easier not to think futures or care about the ones that presented themselves. It was just easier.

"I mean it's your call," said JJ. "But I'll tell you now, leave Holden alone. He did his best, and he's been good to David's family."

"Holden's death is nothing to do with this," Naumenko said dismissively.

"Oh it is. And I'm sure you've been given another reason for having him killed, but I can assure you, Ed Holden's death is everything to do with this, just like mine is, just like Larry Viner's."

Naumenko's brow furrowed as he added up what JJ was saying, his mind working quickly. And within seconds it was there, a look of determination as he said, "Who ordered David's hit?"

"Philip Berg," said JJ simply, and that was sufficient for the moment, an interesting enough name for the countdown to be suspended, a temporary reprieve just as faintly visible as the original warrant. JJ paused, instinctively using his capital, making sure he'd given it time to sink in, then continued, "Probably for Sarkisan but who can say? That's why this crisis came about; in light of his connections with you, he wanted to remove anyone who might have been able to point the finger at him over David Bostridge."

"Interesting," said Naumenko, leaning forward, tapping his index finger lightly against his lips, a metronome's tap as he thought it through. After a minute like that, total silence in the room around them, he said, "Of course, it would be in your interests to make this claim, and in Holden's to tell you the same story."

"Of course," JJ agreed. "Ask yourself one question though. I don't do politics, I don't deal information, I belong to no one. I'm a freelance, a hired gun. So why does Philip Berg want me dead?"

Naumenko answered quickly, suddenly animated, "You know, in all this"—he searched for the right word, savoring it then as he found it—"in all this hullabaloo, that's one question that hadn't occurred to me. But you're right."

He got up and strolled across the room as though suddenly remembering a piece of business he'd meant to attend to. For a few moments then he talked quietly to one of the flunkies, the guy listening intently, nodding, leaving the room as soon as Naumenko dismissed him. Naumenko came back and sat down then, smiling and saying, "Very interesting."

JJ said nothing, knowing there was nothing to respond to; and even though he'd thought he was ready for it a slight nausea was inching into his stomach, his chest, because it didn't look good, the uneasy realization that perhaps Naumenko wasn't saying what he was thinking, that he wasn't buying into JJ's story. There had been no grand pronouncements, no threatening language, but that was how people like Naumenko worked once they'd decided to kill someone, always the same chilling act of disengagement.

They sat there without saying anything, and a few seconds later the door opened again behind where JJ was sitting. Naumenko smiled broadly and said, "Philip, come and join us."

Berg. JJ didn't turn but sensed the surprise off Berg as he reached the sofas.

"Hello, Philip," he said, looking up finally. "I heard you were dead." If Berg had been shocked to see JJ there he'd recovered his composure quickly enough and smiled now as he sat on the arm of the sofa JJ was sitting on. He was wearing a suit, shirt open like Naumenko's, looking like one of those new-breed socialist politicians, glossily corrupt. There was no tan, no sign that he'd been out of the hotel, his hair a richer brown than JJ remembered, like it had been dyed.

"Well as you can see, J, I'm still here, thanks in no small part to Alex."

JJ objected somehow to Berg shortening his name but let it go and then Naumenko said, "JJ's raised some interesting points, Philip."

"Oh really?" Berg was curious, not concerned, the master of the stitch-up, in no doubt as to his own position. JJ thought of Aurianne and did a furtive sweep of the room, wondering if when it came down to the wire he could at least take Berg out with him. He felt his body tense slightly at the thought of it, ready for the first solid signal, certain in his own mind that if he was going he'd take Berg too. The hint of nausea had already gone again and he was just taut now, primed for the strike.

"Yes," Naumenko said, on a roll. "For example, he wants to know why Holden and Viner have been targeted." Berg looked at JJ, outwardly no different from the way he'd been in professional conversations they'd had before.

"It's London business, JJ. Viner and Holden have been working with a faction in Russia—not someone I can disclose here, but Alex has seen the photographic evidence."

"Photographs mean nothing nowadays. Why was Viner killed the way he was? Why were Alex's men sent after Holden? Why wasn't it done in-house?" It was pointless; he knew Berg would have answers, and he knew too that Naumenko would have more reason to want to believe Berg. It was a power play and JJ was just a killer, expendable.

"You know how complicated these things are, J. It's like you. You're the one person in all of this that I regret, but it's precautionary, because of you and Viner. I'm sure you're clean, the fact that you've come here only adds to that, but we can't take the risk. It's nothing personal."

"I think you misunderstand, Philip," Naumenko said. "JJ came here to tell me he killed David Bostridge."

Berg looked at him and then at JJ again, trying to work out what was going on, unnerved possibly by what he saw as JJ's recklessness.

"I don't understand" was all he could find to say, and JJ momentarily wondered if Berg was telling the truth, if it was Holden who'd been lying to him. It just didn't fit though.

"Philip, you disappoint me. Surely you knew?" Naumenko seemed to be enjoying himself but he was definitely involved in more than his own amusement.

"Oh I knew," said Berg, and JJ sensed a chink of light, beginning to think he might have misread the situation, that Naumenko wasn't decided yet on whom he intended to kill. Seeing the opportunity, and suddenly wanting it now more than he'd ever thought he would, he cut in ahead of Naumenko.

"On whose orders? I killed him, Viner gave me the information, but who wanted Bostridge dead?"

"The same Russian faction," replied Berg, like it was an answer he'd hardly needed to give. "Once again, we have evidence to that effect. We don't know if Holden was in the loop or not but it's possible. You know, J, I realize you might have been duped in all of this, and I sympathize, but they were rotten. They were all rotten."

JJ shook his head, showing that he didn't believe it but knowing that his opinion counted for nothing, frustrated again that it all came down to the provenance of the information.

He looked then at Naumenko who smiled and said to him, "You have no more cards to play." And as if he'd read his mind continued, "Not your fault; you're a killer, not an information broker." Turning to Berg, he said casually, "Why didn't you tell me who killed David?"

"I'm sorry?"

"You knew how I felt about David Bostridge. Why didn't you tell me?"

"Because telling you wouldn't have solved anything," Berg said, suddenly earnest, "and frankly, it was a complication I could do without."

Naumenko nodded wistfully and said, "But life is complicated." He made a barely visible gesture and the guy who'd
gone to fetch Berg came back over, putting his hand on Berg's
shoulder. Berg stayed calm but his eyes began to play games.

"Alex," he said, his tone attempting to regain the momentum, but Naumenko looked apologetic, as if there was nothing he could do about it, and answered the point before it
was made, "Please, Philip, let's not make this difficult." Another guy had appeared at Berg's other side, easing him off
the edge of the sofa and pushing him toward a door at the
side of the room, Berg looking like he couldn't catch up
mentally with what was going on.

JJ glanced over, struggling just as much to see how they'd
gotten to that point, getting a glimpse of the bathroom they
were leading Berg into, the door closing behind them. He
turned back to Naumenko who paused for a second and then
said like nothing had happened, "You've met David's family?" JJ nodded. "And?" It took him a moment or two to
bring himself back, trying to catch up with how Naumenko
had come down on his side of the fence, focusing finally on
what he'd been asked about: David Bostridge's family.

"They're great people," he said, smiling at the thought. "A
beautiful wife, attractive kids, smart. His son looks very
much like him."

"Really?"

He thought about it for a while, the silence broken by the
sound of muffled cries and soft blows from beyond the bathroom door. It brought back the memory of Aurianne again,
JJ comforted slightly that Naumenko too had decided Berg
should suffer on his way to the grave. As if he couldn't hear
the disturbance himself Naumenko continued, "I think he'd
grown apart from them somewhat. A source of regret for

him, even of self-recrimination now and then, but he was lost, you know, in his own way, quite lost."

"Aren't we all?" asked JJ. "We're all lost somewhere between freedom and security, trying to find a balance; some people deal with it better than others, that's all."

Naumenko nodded in response, thinking carefully before snapping out of it and saying, "You know, if you'd been anyone else, even after what you've told me, I'd still have killed you for killing David, whether you were just the messenger or not."

JJ nodded and said, "So what marks me out?"

Naumenko paused again, the same muffled sounds from the bathroom, sounding strangely like some quietly forced sex act. He smiled, eyes flicking toward the bathroom door like he'd just heard it for the first time, relishing the irony as he said, "An allowance for dignity, in a very undignified business. That's what it is, why Ed picked you, why I forgive you. And now," he added, moving smoothly on, "what intrigues me just a little bit is that you were the last person to see David alive."

"And why is that intriguing?" He already had an idea why, guessing Naumenko probably knew more about the death than the Moscow police.

"It's a delicate matter. David, as you said, has a beautiful family." He was staring intently at JJ now, reading his expression to catch anything that shifted across it. Carefully then he said, "I received information to suggest he wasn't alone when he was killed."

JJ smiled, because it was clear now that Naumenko had been the one who'd suppressed the existence of the condom, a final act of friendship, just as Holden had performed his in requesting JJ or Lo Bello for the job. If a man's friends were the mark of him, perhaps Bostridge had been more than JJ ever could have guessed from that night.

"He was with a girl, a beautiful girl. I assumed she was a prostitute but Holden thinks it unlikely."

"In this Ed is undoubtedly correct," said Naumenko, who was perhaps best placed to know.

A muted high-pitched cry broke from the bathroom, JJ registering the claustrophobic feel of it as he said, "And she took the icon too."

As with Holden, nothing else he'd said had caused a visible response like the mention of that package. Naumenko looked dumbstruck, spellbound by whatever implications he saw in the information he'd been given. "So it's true," he said, nodding to himself. "Do you know about the icon?"

"Holden told me about it, that it was from Pechorsk, very rare."

"And very beautiful. *The Annunciation* by Theophanes."

"So what's the deal with the girl?"

Naumenko smiled in response, seeing afresh the solution he'd just stumbled upon.

"I heard a rumor," he said theatrically, "that the icon was back in Pechorsk, that it was taken back by the very people we took it from in the first place. Of course"—he leaned back, stretching his arms across the back of the sofa—"it's just a rumor but it's the only rumor I've heard. And if this girl had been a prostitute or if a rival organization had taken it, don't you think I'd have heard a rumor about that too, or an offer to sell at the very least?" JJ didn't respond, thinking it over himself, remembering the way the girl had been as she'd looked for it. "You say this girl was beautiful?"

"Very," replied JJ, trying to picture her but suddenly unable to remember her face.

"Well if you like beautiful Russian girls, this one I think you'll find in Pechorsk. I'm convinced of it. And their icon. And they deserve it, don't you think, if it's true?"

JJ nodded, the fact sinking in that, far from being a prostitute, the girl had been there for a reason beyond the parameters of the world they operated in. And perhaps that explained the way she'd stared at him too, not reaching out but looking at him with pity or contempt or simply with confusion, that he could do what he did so coldly. But, as it had turned out, he hadn't been all he'd seemed that night either, chosen in some parallel universe to perform something akin to a mercy killing. Neither of them had been what they'd seemed.

"Now," said Naumenko brusquely, "perhaps we could discuss business."

"What did you have in mind?"

"Well I take it you no longer feel quite so obliged to London."

"I never did. I have worked exclusively for them, but I intend to change that."

"Good. So you'd consider the occasional job for me?" JJ smiled; an offer of work had been the last thing he'd expected from the meeting.

"On a job-by-job basis, yes, of course. I'm puzzled though." He glanced around the room, listened but could no longer hear anything from the bathroom, an eerily efficient silence. "Why would you need me?"

Naumenko nodded, taking the point but saying, "It would only be occasional. Some jobs are sensitive. It's expedient to have an outsider in these cases. In addition, as Ed knew, people like you are few and far between." He responded quickly to JJ's smile. "You're too modest. You see, I have men in this building who would carry out unspeakable acts, men who have no feelings. Some of them trained, special forces, some of them simply, I suspect, psychopaths. You too have done some unspeakable things, I know this, but what makes you different is that you have a heart—damaged perhaps, I really couldn't say, but still a heart. That," he said emphatically, "gives you an edge these men will never have; it's a very rare thing."

JJ stared at him, no longer smiling, thinking over the double-edged curse Naumenko had just described, something which had been meant to flatter but had left him feeling confused and vaguely wounded instead, and perhaps that in itself proved half the argument, that the edge he had was an understanding of what it was to be hurt.

The bathroom door opened and the first guy stepped out, closing it behind him again. He looked unruffled, still smart and composed, offered a curt nod which Naumenko acknowledged in kind. The guy left the room then.

Naumenko turned back to JJ. "Berg's dead," he said, no trace of emotion, like he was describing someone he'd never met, someone whose death he'd merely read about in the papers. And that was it. Everything that had started a week before, two years before, all of Berg's machinations, finished without fireworks or confrontation in those two simple words.

For all of Naumenko's flowery speaking, there was a bigger truth there too: that hearts were nothing more than machines for pumping blood, and there were countless easy ways of stopping them. Perhaps Berg more than anybody should have known that, and should have been ready, aware that each passing moment was potentially his last.

16

There was a coffee shop on the ground floor, modern and spare, chrome and marble fittings, glass walls giving a view to the lobby, the street door, the elevator and stairs. It was a nice place, the smell of the freshly ground coffee teasing the air, the steam-train sounds of it being made, a quiet background chatter.

Quite a few of the other people in there were on their own, some reading books or newspapers, keeping their own company, others like him, clearly waiting for somebody, glancing toward the lobby now and then. They looked like an even split, locals and tourists, a mix of ages.

And as he sat there a couple of the other people were joined by those they'd waited for, one middle-aged woman greeting another, a young guy kissing his girlfriend, joking about the designer shopping bags she'd brought in. The two women talked urgently once they were together. The girl showed her boyfriend the things she'd bought, opening the bags but not removing the garments.

JJ took it all in but kept looking out to the lobby, patiently waiting, and then he saw who he'd been waiting for, saw him come out of the elevator and through the lobby, heading out into the street, the bodyguard they didn't want killed. He waited till the guy had left and then finished his tea and walked out to the elevator.

Alone, he pressed for eleven and twelve and watched his progress as the numbers lit one by one. When it got to eleven he stepped out, pressing the Open Door button as he left, giving himself an extra twenty seconds to get up the two flights of stairs, heavily carpeted, easy to climb quietly. It was a simple maneuver but effective all the same.

He waited near the top, listening to the elevator's clunking movement inside the wall, and then it stopped and there was a pause and the door opened, and within that second of confusing emptiness he leaned around the corner and took out the guy who was sitting there. He was built like a bull, the useless bulk of a show bodyguard, but he still made no noise as he fell forward and hit the thick pile of the carpet, blood gathering quickly and stickily into the fibers.

JJ strolled into the corridor then like a regular guest, inadvertently catching the other bodyguard listening at Korchilov's door. He pulled away quickly and aimed an unfriendly stare at JJ, keeping eye contact in an attempt to brazen out his own embarrassment. It was a mistake, something the guy realized too late, going for his gun only as JJ fired his first shot. It knocked him backward, his body glancing off the wall, his footing lost as his mind struggled to catch up with what had happened.

Moving quickly, JJ finished him off as he opened the door and walked in to see what the guy had been listening to. Korchilov and a girl were on the bed facing him, the girl on all fours, Korchilov pumping her energetically from behind, both of them moaning, the bed rocking.

JJ didn't even give him a chance to break his rhythm, putting a bullet straight into his forehead. Blood spurted out over the girl's back before Korchilov fell backward and lay crumpled against the headboard, a look of amazement on his face, like he was too young, too alive and powerful for this to happen to him.

The girl looked like a child, confused, unsure why Korchilov had suddenly withdrawn. JJ glanced over at the coffee table, enough pills and powder on it to have had a full-scale party, and when he looked at the girl he could see she was tripping on cocktails. She clambered off the bed and stared at Korchilov for a second, then at JJ, puzzled but too dulled to work it out. She looked pretty, vulnerable, the kind of girl who'd been unlucky enough to be born with good looks and nothing else.

She stared at him like someone in a hall of mirrors, trying to make sense of what she could see, her pupils dilated. And then she seemed to focus on him, battling through the haze, her mouth moving like she was trying to say something. He shot her in the chest, the impact throwing her backward like a cast-aside toy, and shot her again in the head as soon as she'd hit the floor.

He left straight away then, walking along the corridor, getting the elevator back to the ground floor. He walked through the lobby, no one paying any attention to him, a businessman buttoning up against the cold. He walked out of the hotel, out into the busy city, the gray-skied morning, the upper reaches of some buildings half lost in the mist.

• • •

Early the next morning the mist was still there, obscuring the roof of the city, but it was a different kind of mist, snow flurries falling from it like ticker tape, dying dirtily on the street under tires and feet. After an hour on the train though, it was real snow, too much to be trodden away, swaddling bands on the world, enveloping everything.

The mood on the train was excitable, sociable, JJ letting himself get drawn into conversation now and then with other passengers. There were a lot of people heading up for the skiing, the weather keenly discussed, the condition of the snow they were passing through, how it was looking for the days ahead.

The snow was falling as constantly as it had all day but the drive at the other end was still okay, even the road that led to the Copley cleared, the inn and half-hidden village below looking even more picturesque but fresher too somehow, more elemental, reminding him of home a little, the same seasonal transition.

It was the third time he'd been here. When he'd left the first time he hadn't been certain about going back, and he'd been even less so in the weeks following. But he'd gone back, had taken that leap, and had found himself counting off the days then in the back of his mind till he could make another trip.

It was partly the place—he was developing an attachment to its rhythms—partly the people—Susan Bostridge's easy hospitality, the constant flow of guests, their kindest sides to the fore, people who were essentially decent, the way most people were in the world, a fact it was easy to forget sometimes in what he did.

It was mainly for Jem, though, that he went back there, a tightly woven friendship developing between them, JJ constantly reminded of her when he wasn't there, in the details of faces, in the things he saw. Maybe it wasn't healthy but he didn't think about it, conscious only that he wanted to be there when he wasn't, and that he felt more at ease in her company than he had with anyone else for a long time. What was there to think about in it?

Kathryn met him in the lobby when he arrived, fussing over him, asking him questions like she'd known him for years. A moment later Susan came out and pecked him on the cheek, saying casually, "Lovely to see you again, JJ. How was Christmas?"

"Fine thanks. With my family, you know, quiet."

She smiled and said longingly, turning to Kathryn, "Wouldn't you just love the holidays in Switzerland?"

"Oh yes, how romantic," said the older woman, and JJ was puzzled about what they thought Switzerland could offer them over and above what they had.

"And speaking of Christmas, we saw Tom over the holidays. He wants to know why you haven't been in touch."

JJ smiled, appreciating the way Tom had played along with the idea of them being great friends, and said then, "No excuse really, but I have been busy, a lot of work over here as you know. Then a friend of mind had a baby, so . . . And I've moved since I last saw you."

"Oh?"

"Yeah, into the mountains."

Susan smiled at Kathryn again and said with a knowing smile, "Christmas in Switzerland!" Changing tone then she said, "Now, I'll get your key. Oh, and you'll have dinner with us tonight?"

"I'd love to."

"Good. And Jem's waiting in the lounge to see you."

"Your lounge?"

"No, the communal one; she didn't want to miss you when you arrived." He smiled indulgently, showing the right face.

"In which case," he said, "I ought to pop in and see her now." He moved his bags over near the stairs. Susan drifted off and came back with his key, saying as she gave it to him, "By the way, don't mention Freddie."

"He broke her heart?" JJ asked, grimacing slightly.

"She broke his, which shows how wrong a mother can be. She feels guilty about it."

He smiled and walked away to the lounge.

The room was overrun with the white light of the snow outside, a dreamlike haziness on everything it touched, on the furniture, on Jem where she sat reading. For a moment she appeared oblivious, a ghost; then she looked up and saw him, gave him an immediate reactive smile.

"Hey," she said and jumped up like she was about to throw her arms around him but stopped herself short, suddenly conscious of his physical presence, her own body language falling back awkward and shy.

"It's good to see you," he said, smiling as if to acknowledge the difficulty of how to greet each other, finally kissing her on the cheek, the girl blushing slightly as they sat down.

"So, are you here on like, business or pleasure?"

"Business in New York, pleasure here." He noticed a newspaper on a table nearby, folded open on a page bearing the Korchilov story, reminded of Lenny and Dee Kaplan by the sight of it. "Actually the business in New York wasn't essential, more of an excuse. I wanted to see what this place looked like in the winter, check out some of the cross-country trails you were talking about."

"We could go in the morning," she replied quickly, adding, "I mean, whenever, but like, if you don't have anything else to do."

"Like I said, it's what I came for. What about skis?"

She looked bashful again, saying, "I've kind of taken care of that."

"Thanks," he said, nodding. "Tomorrow morning it is then."

He looked at her for a second or two, half smiling, until finally she said, "What!"

"Nothing," he said innocently. "Only, I heard you broke up with Freddie."

She whooped with mortified laughter, covering her face, repeating again and again, "I don't believe it. No, I don't believe it," surging into the details then, all the teenage drama in its gory detail, the easiness drifting back between them.

They left about an hour after breakfast the following morning. There were plenty of other people around at first on the marked trails, but they fell away into isolation as Jem took JJ farther into her own territory, routes through the woods that only someone like her would know.

For a lot of the time they said nothing, a silence almost demanded of them by the pillows of snow, hollow woods, earth-hugging sky. And when they spoke their voices carried on the crisp air, an intimate winter acoustic.

There wasn't much to say anyway, all their memories of skiing cross-country already familiar to each other, a whole evening spent talking about it on his previous trip to the inn. It was almost as if they'd skied together before.

After a couple of hours they began skiing steadily up-ward, long zigzags up a deep wooded slope. At one point she turned, her breath short, and said, "This is a tough climb, but it's like *so* worth it when we get to the top."

He nodded, not saying anything, leaving the fading trace of her voice to linger there.

He spoke when they got to the top though, a simple "Wow" as he looked over the expanse of the untouched snowfield stretching out flat below them, more wooded hills on the far side, nothing between them but an untouched white bedsheet of snow, an inviting emptiness.

"Beautiful, isn't it?"

"Stunning," he agreed.

They stood there for a couple of minutes, just staring at it, a whiteness that seemed to swallow up vision and sound. Fi-nally she said slowly, "I used to ski a lot with my dad when I was a kid. A little kid. A few years ago I found this place on my own, like, nearly the end of the season, and I just found it. So I told my dad about it, and he said we'd come here to-gether sometime, so I could show it to him."

He looked at her, her face still, the only time she'd spoken about her father since that first day, apparent now that it had been something she'd wanted to talk about sooner or later. And though his nerves were bristling it was something he'd wanted too, despite the discomfort it would carry within it.

"He never came," said JJ, sensing it in her voice, knowing it from the time scale.

She shook her head in response but added, "Not just be-cause of that. Maybe if he'd lived, like, another ten years, we'd have come here together. We were kind of growing apart, you know; I wasn't his little girl anymore."

The thought of the girl in Moscow hemorrhaged into his mind, and JJ said in reflex, "That's the worst thing about death, it has a way of catching you just as life's overtaken you."

She looked at him like she was thinking about it, possibly not understanding, then looked ahead and said, "You'd lost someone close when you first came here."

"Close," he said, thinking of his already distant memory of Aurianne, "but I don't think I lost . . ." He ground to a halt, suddenly realizing what she'd just said, what she'd meant by lost. "You know about Aurianne?"

"Not just Aurianne . . ." She turned again and met his gaze, her eyes searching, something building up behind them. Finally she produced a weak smile and said, "I've wanted to tell you for a long time."

He stared at her, numb, ambushed, the fact only slowly sinking in. He was confused too by the way she looked, compassion where there should have been anger, hostility. JJ managed to say only, "How?"

"Ed," she replied matter-of-factly. "Ed and me have always been kind of close. He trusts me, thinks I can deal with the truth and stuff, whatever. He told me about Dad a few weeks after it happened, even like, about him knowing and everything, about asking for the right guy to do it if it had to be done." She looked away from him, staring out over the snowfield, JJ's mind stalled by her composure, by the fact that a girl of her age had carried this around with her, shocked too that Holden had burdened her with it, a weight of knowledge that was an act of cruelty in itself. "Then last September, he told me that guy was coming to the inn, that he was coming to help him with a problem. He didn't tell me until like, Christmas, you know, what the problem was. But you were the guy."

She turned briefly, long enough to offer him another fleeting half smile, a nod to the strangeness of things. And as he stood there looking back at her he thought of the way she'd looked at him on the stairs that first time, and of her taking him to her father's grave. It all seemed to add up now, the way she'd been with him.

"What about the others?"

She shook her head without looking at him. "They don't know. Ed might seem flaky but he has people pretty well figured."

They stood in silence until JJ said, "I don't know what to say. I don't . . ."

She turned again, saying quietly, "Don't. It had to happen. It happens. Maybe one day we can talk about it some more." She paused, her eyes fixing him, her face ruddy with the cold air, her lips full and red. "I'm glad it was you, that's all. I'm glad it was you."

He offered her the same smile she'd given him, inadequate but the only response he could manage, his heart overfull with blood, his thoughts flooded, sodden with knowledge for which he could never have readied himself, not that she knew, but that she understood, that she forgave him or didn't even see a need to forgive him. Without being aware of doing it then, he took his glove off, watching his own hand as it lifted and wiped from her cheek the single tear that had traced its path there, her face cold against his fingers, Jem smiling a little as his hand fell away again.

"Shall we move on?" she asked a few seconds later, as if they were done with it, or possibly as if she still didn't want to dwell on it; the difficulty of the journey her own mind had taken to that point was something he couldn't even guess at. He nodded but then, catching up with himself, felt like he

had to say something else, at least something, to stop feeling
the fraud he was by accepting her vision of him.

"Jem, I don't know how Ed painted me; he's a good guy,
he means well. But I kill people, that's all I do, your dad just
one more job, and it doesn't matter what light you put on it,
I didn't do anything good there in Moscow. All I did was kill
someone; there's no goodness in it, none."

She smiled once more, this time like it was JJ who didn't
understand, and said, "I think you're wrong. I think sometimes there's a goodness where you'd least expect it." She
paused then and added, "Let's not talk about it. I just
wanted you to know, to know that I understand, and, well,
you know, that it doesn't change anything. I'm glad it was
you. That's all."

He nodded thoughtfully at the repeated phrase, an understanding taking root between them, that it was enough for
now, that it was at least in the open where they'd needed it,
no longer the obstacle it would have been whether she'd
known about it or not.

They stood in silence then as he put his glove back on,
glancing at each other once more before pushing forward,
down the gentle slope ahead of them, pushing on into the
open spaces of the snowfield, heading into the elusive peace
of being lost on the winter landscape.

He still wanted to speak at first, to tell her again that she
was wrong, or to ask her to explain how she could feel that
way, how she could find it within herself not to hate him for
who he was. But he said nothing, humbled by her, knowing
that he wouldn't have been able to find the words.

It was hard for him to accept, this belief of hers that there
was good in him where he could see none himself, but it
didn't mean she was wrong, perhaps only that she was look-

ing in a different way, seeing more clearly. Because he had killed Bostridge cleanly, the thing he'd been chosen for, and maybe the goodness of this friendship had arisen out of that, and the goodness of everything that had come to him with it, a sense that there was something to head for, a reason to keep going.

So he kept silent, wondering how they could ever speak about anything else again, how they'd move on to another carefree subject. Once they were lost on the flat of the snowfield though, she let herself glide to a stop, and as he slowed and turned to see if she was okay he saw her smiling, almost laughing with exhilaration, like she'd already shed it, something she'd carried from the day they'd met.

"Isn't this great?" she said, holding her arms out at the landscape, her words steaming skyward in vapor trails.

He nodded, easing back toward her, and said, "It's what downhillers don't understand."

"I know." She looked around, shaking her head as if in disbelief at the hazy expanse of snow surrounding them. "I've wanted to show someone this place for so long. I mean, it's like a miracle, you know, that it's so beautiful, but like, so transitory. I mean, I don't think I believe in God or anything, but this makes you kind of realize, I guess, that . . ."

Her words fell away, like she couldn't pin down what she wanted to say, and JJ said, "That we're part of something bigger, that there's a reason for things."

She smiled, staring at him. "That's it," she said, adding with a note of curiosity, "Do you believe in God? I don't know why I didn't ask before."

"No, I don't, but I see this, and I understand why people do."

She nodded in agreement, looking around, awestruck by

its beauty, JJ doubly awestruck that he was there with her. She pointed then and said, "Do you wanna go all the way across?" He nodded and turned and they moved off in silence again, talking only sparingly.

And as they headed into the white escape, he became lulled by the feel of the snow, the sound of their skis as they sheared its surface, the cold air as it streamed against his face. His thoughts began to die away, lost in each passing winter moment, until his mind was stripped bare, and then in that vacuum a simple truth arose, from something he'd said to her just a few minutes before, that some people saw all of this and explained it with a belief in God.

It made him realize something he'd almost lost sight of, that maybe some other good too had come of that killing in Moscow. Because he had to believe now, as Naumenko did, that hidden in another winter landscape, a continent away, already sunk in darkness, was an icon, beautiful perhaps, valuable, an Annunciation. It meant more to those people than it ever could have elsewhere, representing to them what it did, representing everything.

They'd kept it through centuries of history's ebb and flow before its theft, refusing to let it go even then, their faith making them determined to retrieve it from people whose motives were alien to them. And at the last, perhaps only a day away from losing it forever, it had been found and taken back.

That was where JJ had played his part, because it had been returned to the place it belonged by a girl who'd seen him kill a man, a witness, someone who by rights should never have survived herself. She'd seen inside him though, had seen something which in her own silent way she'd tried to communicate.

And at the time he hadn't understood, but he'd been moved by her all the same, a girl he'd had no reason to spare but who, in a moment of weakness, he'd chosen not to kill. It was a scant gift but all he'd had to offer, and on that night perhaps, few could have offered much more.

ABOUT THE AUTHOR

KEVIN WIGNALL, thirty-four, was born in Herentals, Belgium, where his father was stationed as a soldier. After living in Northern Ireland and Germany, the family settled in a small town in the west of England where he still lives. He graduated with a degree in politics and international relations from Lancaster University. Certain only that he didn't want a regular job after leaving university, he traveled, campaigned, wrote on the environment, and taught English as a foreign language. Having always written, it was during his brief stint as an English teacher that he began work on his first novel, *People Die*.